OROTUND

OROTUND

COLLECTED SHORT STORIES

VOLUME TWO

BY BP GREGORY

ISBN 978 0 6457319 8 9

ACKNOWLEDGMENTS

Orotund cover image by Alex Malikov.

Strangers cover image by Aprilphoto. Glory cover image by PaulPaladin. The Self Made Man cover image by Vlue. Submerged cover image by AlexussK. Stow cover image by Leszek Kobusinski. Economy cover image by Vendla Stockdale. Mould cover image by Andy Dean Photography. Terry cover image by Sofiaworld. All courtesy of Shutterstock.

Something for Everything cover image by Extradeda, The Town cover images by Pavelr and Tim Bird, Orotund cover image by Alex Malikov, Lunchbox cover images by kamontad999 and Sakdinon Kadchiangsaen, and Visit the Website image by Peter Dedeurwaerder all courtesy of Shutterstock.

Mould appeared on creepypasta.com in 2014.

Stow was written for Kym, and her deep intense passion for scrapbooking. And Tim, for asking me to prod and poke at the original mystery Promise sprang from, leading inexorably to Stow.

In writing Submerged I have to thank my perfectly normal and lovely neighbours, who in all innocence inquired as to whether I'd been murdered, and then chuckled that it would make a great story idea.

With Economy I'd like to acknowledge my lovely sister, who I once saw fly down a church aisle like a streak of lighting. Thank you for proving that you should always proceed at your own pace.

Content Advisory

These stories feature adult themes including child abuse, child neglect, claustrophobia, loss of a loved one, mental health issues, paedophilia, prostitution, sexually explicit scenes, terrorism, and traumatic death. They may not be suitable for all readers.

STORIES

strangers

BP Gregory

a short story

STRANGERS

THIS STINKS, thought Denny morosely, like some mother's group setting him up, the divine angels of society's secret vile justice. The little girl, the object of his attention had LOST stamped all over her, pale little lip quivering. And nobody was doing anything. Not one of these stern upright folk; folk who always found a way to pass the word about him, no matter how many times he moved. His crap just lived in boxes these days, those boxes getting fewer and fewer.

Nobody shuttling back and forth on their very important business so much as glanced down, but of course Denny couldn't help noticing the little girl lost, it was his sodding curse. Even with the injections that had just made him sick at first rather than better, and then killed off most of his, well, *stuff*, the child was all lit up: she glowed amidst the heedless sea of grey faces and grey suits. She was all that was real, more than real, and no science or witchdoctory ever helped.

Talking to some poor kid, any child, violated his parole in a big ol' way: and wasn't that what the world at large was holding its breath for? Likely some righteous keen eyes had already noticed he'd been staring, staring for far too long, and he ought to just move along same as all these other good folk who didn't see the skinny legs jutting all knobbly from under the comically big backpack. Didn't notice the big, baffled and increasingly tearful eyes contemplating some scrap of paper in her small hand.

Besides, nothing Denny had ever done ever turned out good for anyone; and with that familiar deep old shame he admitted he was a jinx, a curse, just like his brother said. Ought to be locked away for everyone's protection.

But now there was this girl. One busy fellow actually knocked the kid as he hurried by, nearly sending her over: no apology, nothing; and for Denny that was it. He crossed the road to her, heart pounding. *This is suicide, suicide!* Alarms would already be being whispered into phones.

'Hello.' Stupid, but what else do you say? Doubtful eyes looked up at him, and he found it hard to breathe. She knew what he was, she knew, she must know. Children had a sixth sense, like cats, and had never liked him. 'You lost?'

The girl offered him the piece of paper. Almost as scared as she was Denny took it, careful not to touch her hand: you didn't touch kids, oh no no. Not even with the injections.

It was a map. Almost looked like it'd been drawn for her by another child. A big red arrow pointed to a building, with the crude glyph of a book.

'The library? This is where you're trying to go?'

The girl waited and Denny expanded under a massive bloom of relief: he knew where the library was, he knew! Hunkering down he pointed up the street, unsure of what the girl could actually see above all the people hurrying here and there. Not a lot, it seemed. 'Go four blocks that way, and take a left at the building with the big flag.'

Time was up; his jackals would be closing in, ready to save the day. No more strikes, Denny. You're out. He could almost feel the beating claustrophobia of their fists and shoes already, which was a strange relief. He'd take it over the never ending stares, hateful letters, and windows broken in his progression of shabby government housing flats.

But the kid took the map back with a grateful relief of her own, scurrying away down the street through the heedless ranks of those closing in. And Denny crossed his arms and thought defiantly to himself: it was worth it.

It was Violet who saw the girl next. Violet, who bitterly missed hearing the name from her birth certificate, wasn't due on shift 'til three when the hole opened but that didn't stop the tired old fuckers lining up out front like cheap sex was some kind of celebrity. She sat on the curb and smoked blues to drown the stench and scowled sourly at them, shuffling their worn out hush puppies and fumbling pension money in crabbed fingers. And if her 'tude meant Mr Happy wasn't going to play—well whoop-di-doo, they had to pay at the door regardless.

Violet always noticed other people's little girls, always punishing herself with a hurt sneer 'cause she hated looking at them. She loathed that prompting of days she could no longer remember: tutus and praise and running free with a chest as flat as a board. Days of doting parents (two!) who drummed into your little skull that the only requirement for beauty was to be a good person, a futile effort at getting the concept across before the world put lie to it.

Soon enough this little pretty struggling under the enormous backpack would sprout, and society would vacuum pack her titties and put them on sale. That first heady sip of power over the gangly boys in school and she'd be hooked, just in time for the kicker—it was all a lie! It didn't last, and with all the excitement she'd missed every damn opportunity to make anything else of herself. Finally washed up in a nightmare like this, where every pump of a client's flabby hips drove dreams of home further from recall.

What was a kid doing out wandering this neighbourhood anyhow? Where were the parents who were s'posed to hold reality at bay just that little bit longer—this was rubbing the poor kid's nose in the filth!

Worse news. Usually disposed toward the pretence that each other didn't exist, the gaggle of old fuckers had noticed the girl and were muttering away. None with the juice left in his saggy old balls to take the job on himself, but maybe if they spread the responsibility nice and thin amongst their ranks ..?

'Fucktards.' Violet crushed out her cigarette and groaned to her feet. That was just what the girl needed—visions of things to come.

'Hey. Where ya goin', kid?'

At the swimming eyes that turned up to hers, Violet's jaded heart almost broke. She wanted to snatch the kid up and run far, far from here, take her someplace safe and pure and happy that just didn't exist.

The little girl held up her pathetic map, which by now was getting a bit smudged and teary. Perhaps she'd just been too young for Denny's well-meaning directions, to tell left from right. Violet studied the paper and squeezed an elbow into her side to pacify the savage sympathy in her chest—after all these stifling years, it was finally set free. Poor little blighter probably left home all optimistic, convinced she was a big enough girl to do this trip on her own; then the world set its big boot down on that vanity.

She traced her finger across the kid's map. 'Here, see? You go here—then there.' The solemn little face gazed up at her: *yes ma'am, thankyou ma'am*. She looked like the sort of little girl who might say "ma'am". Tears forestalled for now—although they'd certainly come another day.

'Well, off you go, then.'

It was soft, but Violet couldn't help feeling just that little bit warmer as she watched the small figure trot away, map clenched firm in one determined fist. Maybe she was going somewhere after all.

The final leg of the journey fell to Sam. He was writing up the rest of a traffic violation, wearily trying to ignore the shouted "Fuck you pig!" as the perp pulled away. It really wasn't worth the extra paperwork; and he was so sick of paperwork.

All he'd ever wanted was to help people, and the badge had seemed the most logical route there. But how could you help anyone when you came slam up against a wall of nasty suspicious people who cheated all the time, who exploded in outrage should you question their purity *especially* when they were in the wrong, and who were convinced in their horrible little minds that you were out to get them when really they'd got themselves without any help at all.

The people, the community he'd so wanted to assist never seemed so far away. Sam was lost.

It hurt him to see a child so obviously looking for something, but who wouldn't come up to the policeman standing *right here* to ask for directions. Mired in newspaper scandals of corruption and drugs that was just what mothers told their kids these days—never trust a cop. Better to chance it with strangers.

But Sam was always sure to do his job, even when it hurt him, *particularly* when it hurt, because if he didn't up and do the right thing you could be sure nobody else would.

He knelt to come somewhat close to the girl's eye level—God, she was so tiny! And what was with these ridiculous great bags the schools loaded them up with these days? He could see bobbly knees trembling in those pale stick legs; the bulky thing probably outweighed her. He'd had *meals* that outweighed the poor kid, all strapped and buckled into her bag like it were some medieval torture device.

Her family was probably dirt poor. This massive sack of books, instead of a laptop. Both parents would be bent to the wheel at work, unable to escort their tiny daughter around town no matter how much they longed to. If she had no siblings she'd grow up alone, assembling her own sparse breakfasts and likely dinners, too in an empty home while ma and pa clocked overtime, missing their daughter's childhood as they struggled to make ends meet *for her*. That was the cruel part.

Not for the first time Sam promised himself that if he had them, *his* kids would enjoy a parent at home. They wouldn't have to endure the loneliness and risk of solitary trips around town. Which was of course preposterous: nobody had money to live that dream, and his certainly wasn't the career to be making long term commitments to anyone. When it came to children, Sam suspected he had already missed the boat.

At least he might make this lass' day a little brighter. Assuming she didn't spit in his face and flee into the crowd, that was. 'Hello there. What's your name?'

Tiny fingers twisted shyly. Sam could already tell he wasn't getting a response but that was ok, things could be going worse. He tapped his name badge. 'My name's Sam. Officer Sam.' He paused awkwardly: it made him sound like a cartoon character … which he didn't mind, actually. Pretending for the moment to belong to a cleaner, brighter reality. 'You look like you could use a little help.'

She hesitantly proffered the map. Good God, somebody sent their child out onto the street with *this*? No wonder the poor mite got lost; it looked like it had been drawn with crayon! 'The library, huh? Well you did a real good job hon, almost made it on your own. It's right around the corner.'

The little girl glowed with the praise, and Sam came to a quick decision. 'Come on, then—I'll walk you there. I can even carry that backpack for you; it looks heavy.'

His reward was a solemn little smile as she struggled out of the straps, which lightened his day considerably. This was why he'd become a policeman! He was helping!

Finally free of her burden the little girl stretched in relief, and Sam hefted its weight with wonder. Tough little cookie, he couldn't believe she'd managed to stagger about under that thing. *No child of mine*, he swore to himself. His kids would be soft and happy and hopeful. They would make the future a better place.

The two of them companionably walked the sidewalk together, past the splatters of vomit that never seemed to wash away, past the panhandlers squatting in it—no point busting them for a permit; they couldn't afford the fee anyhow, unless a torrent of foul mouthed abuse could be considered currency. As though sensing Sam's darkening thoughts the little girl walked closer. When her frail hand crept tentatively into his, he felt his worn spirit begin to soar.

The library's steps were cluttered with students. All reading, talking on their phones, laughing and sipping coffee in this brief burst of sunshine between classes. Hand in hand Sam and the little girl threaded their way to the top and entered cool air conditioning through big double doors that had been flung wide all day to welcome the curious in.

Upon finally reaching her destination the explosives in the little girl's backpack ignited. For kilometres around all of the people and their worries and cares were promptly incinerated in a blast of golden light.

GLORY

STUDENTS WERE DISCOURAGED from venturing into the park's public toilet. Of course they all knew, in whispers and titters, it was because of the hole. Not much bigger than a fist, it looked to have been brutally bashed right through the third cubicle's wall. That poky little cubicle with its crooked door was the crux of a whole slew of lurid urban legends.

Even girls from the neighbouring campus seemed in on it; shocked the hell out of Jack the first time he overheard them giggling and carrying on. Girls were supposed to be nicer than that. Why should they know *anything* about the men's toilet?

Men's. Not boys'. Jack supposed aspiration might explain why he'd taken to defiantly pissing where he oughtn't to be. Got to be a nice little ritual: his stream drumming against the metal trough, the sound booming in the icy concrete room.

The wind whooped about the verdant green oval outside. Like the excited squabbling of gulls on a distant cliff, he could faintly discern the shrieks of various district sport teams hashing it out. All of whom'd be doing peachy without him, thank you very much.

The toilet block was a good place to be alone. Like some private sleepy island, where hectic summer was barred. Where Jack could almost feel calm, tucked away from the fizzing, bubbling world that made him want to spring from his skin and go racing for the horizon.

Still, while going about his business he made sure to stand with his back to the infamous third cubicle. Not *scared*, as such. More vaguely ashamed, in case someone looked in. What lurked back there wasn't anything a nice kid wanted to go showing interest in.

So the sly whisper that one day came dripping and slithering from the hole's dark maw almost did manage to tweak him right out of his skinny hide.

'Hey! Bring it 'ere, boy.'

It was a thick voice, clotted and low. Furtive in a way adults shouldn't ever be. You couldn't help picturing the ponderous bristled bulk it must emanate from.

All of the hair instantly raised up on Jack's flinching neck like cactus spines. Although a reasonably solid wall loomed between them he was too terrified to so much as twitch.

'Bring it 'ere, then. Go on. It'll feel *good.*'

The gutter-voice paused, as though considering what might tempt a nice boy. Perhaps, horribly, it was trying to remember its own childhood.

'Ya c'n pretend it's anyone. Like all them giiirlies, is runnin' 'round out there. Ya like one o' them girlies?'

Wetter and closer, the mouth pressed eagerly against the hole with a flickering tongue. That great misshapen head trying to squeeze its way through like sausage meat.

Of course he liked one of them! Who wouldn't?

'It c'ld be *her* doin' it to ya. How'd ya like that?'

Jack forced himself around. He had to, to face the door. No sense fleeing hysterically through the dim room without looking, which was all he wanted to do. Likely smack against a wall and knock himself silly. No telling what might happen with him laid out cold.

His portal back into the nice safe world blared so brightly into the room it was a rectangle cut from bleeding light. The afterimage blinded his eyes everywhere he dared look. A temporary, scrabbling panic until vision returned.

The hole, though. The hole was dark. Fathomless, like it drilled through to nowhere. No hint of what skulked behind there, crooning its sweet nothings.

It was a no brainer, right?

Except for the burning enticement of the voice's next slippery words, laid out precisely like a trail of sweets. It was a prospect that unbelievably impelled Jack *toward* the cubicle, his poor legs trembling so badly he was sure any second to be spilled across the hard, clay-smelling floor.

'Ya c'ld be *makin'* her do it.'

Because that's what it came down to, wasn't it? The only way any of those girls would ever be accessible to *him*.

One more step and he was there, like a man on the moon.

Gooseflesh rippled and crept in shivering fingers up Jack's tender, bared stomach; in his fright he'd neglected to cover himself. The skin of his stones crawled as though appalled.

Glancing down Jack saw the little curling hairs tremble in a puff of stray breeze from the other side of the hole. Or, if it was the satisfied chuffing of breath that he heard, then why on earth did it feel so dreadfully cold?

A moment of hesitation. Then, before he could chicken out,

he quickly stuffed himself through.

As promised came warmth, a wet cavity. A hot mouth that closed over his unhappy, shrivelling little nugget and flogged it to instant, thrumming attention. A jaded mouth that knew exactly what it was after, and pursued it mercilessly.

Jack groaned, spreadeagled against the gritty wall with his strides puddled about his feet and socks still yanked comically high. That voice was sodding right. This felt so *good!*

Distantly he caught the shrill calls of the girls out on the football oval. So far off, it was like they frolicked on another planet. In fact they might as well, for all the luck he'd had. Each had their charms, but luminous unobtainable Beth most of all.

Beth's long legs flashing in the afternoon glow. Sometimes she skimmed carelessly here and there, like a dragonfly. Then suddenly she became a sleek muscled predator intently chasing down the ball. Warm thundering life incarnate.

Jack scarce had words for all this. What good were fucking words, anyhow? This, *this* feeling was what he'd been made for! Wound up and set ticking, just to give himself over to it.

Before he knew it he was jerking and spasming, drowning that secret mouth. Smothering a voice that chortled and gurgled its pleasure, as Jack yanked up his shorts and fled. Casting only one wide-eyed glance back: Christ, he'd left the cubicle door open! Anyone might have strolled in and seen!

Over the next few weeks Jack tried to uphold the fiction that he only dared the public toilet for an irresistible piss. At least at first.

He haunted the park.

His pa was baffled but declared himself dutifully proud at the variety of sports his boy was suddenly keen on. Blissfully unaware of how Jack sat parked on the sidelines every day, swilling bottle after bottle of electrolyte water from the corner store 'til his eyeballs were floating. Glumly watching the girls shriek and flap about.

Girls like those, Jack wished so fervently to possess, but was puzzled what he'd do should he snag one. Dress her up, maybe?

Vivid imagination saw him posturing long smooth limbs against a diorama in formal, ritual movements, like one of his brattish sister's tea parties.

While another part of Jack, dark and urgent, asserted he knew very well what he'd do with her.

So very well.

Jack's parents went and threw a birthday party he sure didn't ask for.

There was even a big football-shaped cake on the table in honour of his new interests. Crammed so full of frustration with the lot of them that he was practically vibrating, on the verge of flying apart, Jack seized his first opportunity to slip away.

Away from the bright lights of his laughing festive family, who were busy pulling party-poppers in each others' faces and carrying on like some species of idiot who didn't give a damn about anything. Into darkness and a whistling cold that made him wish he'd brought a coat.

Jack went jogging through the empty night to the park.

He didn't generally see a whole lot of jogging in his day-to-day. His breath pounded harsh in his ears, but gradually as it worked through his system his roiling blood began to settle.

What am I doing? he wondered. *Just what the fuck am I thinking?*

The park was a different place by night. It lolled out

bonelessly, much bigger, its geometry adult and strange. The streetlights burned few and far between, and it occurred to Jack, *I could be robbed out here.*

I could get murdered.

There'd be no living with shame should his rellies sniff things out, that was for fucking sure. Even the idea made his gut wobble.

Good old Jack, discovered the next morning in the sordid public toilet. Sprawled face-down with his pants tangled around knobby ankles like they'd kept him from fleeing.

A deviant scene to be unearthed by the poor little juniors, they were always first on the field. The early bird gets the emotional scarring. So take a good gander, you toddling fuckers. Know all that stuff they promised? *This* is what truly waits up ahead.

Kids shrieking for teachers, for adults who were in cahoots with this heartless world. Adults who'd sigh reprovingly and bring in cops, the press, whoever. See there's a moral to be learned here folks, so step right up!

And the hole lit up. All lurid and leering in the flash of a newspaper's camera.

In which case it'd be *great* to be dead.

Nevertheless Jack continued, wretchedly unable to resist. Across crisp gravel to soft, soundless grass, his nose full of vegetative tang. His bare arms seemed to be steaming in the cold.

But hey, were he quick enough he could hopefully flit on back before his parentals lit the candles and realised their little boy was missing his Happy Birthday.

Solemn-faced Beth drifted briefly behind Jack's eyes as he jiggled and thrust, panting frantically. But the artificial light overhead glowed dull and leprous, crawling with insects. Every chill surface branded his skin. And with the drain in the floor backed up, the close room was dank with raw piss.

He couldn't hold onto the promise of her, not in a place like this. Here there was only the hole.

In fact, Jack never found her again.

That was also the night Jack noticed he had bits missing.

His scrawny pelvis was ringed in a proud array of scabs and scrapes from the unyielding concrete. Looked like he'd been trying to fuck some damn pissed-off tomcat. And at first he reckoned this was more of the same.

Then he prayed, urgently, that it was.

With his pyjama bottoms raked down Jack switched on his bedside rocket lamp, which he'd vowed to never outgrow. Moving quick and furtive, lest his ma pop in for a goodnight kiss.

What he found illustrated very clearly that Jack'd never been scared before. Not even close; he'd only ever been pretending.

Because now he actually swooned, in a fever of nauseating panic. Crashed sideways into the rocket and smashed its ignition for good.

Probably for the best. He really couldn't stand to see anymore.

Still in mortal dread of discovery and too traumatised to revise that priority, Jack clumsily tugged his pants up in the dark and crawled beneath the doona. Trembling and moaning quietly to himself all the while. Even curled in a knot he couldn't seem to get warm.

Now he understood how fluttering birds died of a shock they just couldn't recover from. His hands and feet knocked about like senseless lumps of ice, and he didn't know how he'd ever crawl out there again.

The tip of Jack's dick was gone.

That's what he'd seen as he doubled over in curious inspection, trying to understand the visual difference.

Not bitten or severed, mind, which would have sent him wailing to the emergency room.

Just … gone.

A couple of days trying to pretend it wasn't happening garnered Jack quite what you'd expect.

All the while, what ailed him steadily worsened. It was more than only the tip now; God, how he longed for the days when it'd been just the tip! He was consumed by an utter creeping panic, going about his routine with a scream swelling his head desperately like a balloon.

After dithering outside the sickbay for hours Jack tried spilling his bewildered saga to the nurse. Or at least what few parts he could bear to spit out. The worst of the tale jammed in his throat, too toxic for extraction no matter how he tugged and convulsed.

Could he have just shown her? Funnily enough, it turned out while Jack was A-ok with jamming his junk through a mystery wall, he was too precious to drop his dacks in the office of a mildly perturbed school nurse.

The nurse shifted uncomfortably, clearly not keen on having the door locked. 'Well this really isn't my area. But I'm quite concerned to be hearing your communication troubles. I hardly see what's the great drama in speaking to girls your age; I mean, they're just people. You've got to get this idea they're some kind of mystic icons out of your head, or you'll always be terrified.'

No, Jack thought dismally. I can't imagine you see it at all.

What he wanted more than anything was somebody to stop him. Because he still guzzled those electrolytes, in such quantities he'd joined a recycling program, too.

He just couldn't keep away from the park.

Jack couldn't stand to look down at himself. The very idea of a glimpse made him vomit wretchedly, so he went to great pains not to: dressed in the dark, showered carefully with his eyes closed.

For a brief peaceful period he lost touch with himself, a floating head connected to nothing. And considered it a blessing.

Until the rainy afternoon he heard the guttural, thickened demand, 'Bring it *closer*,' and realised he'd nothing left anymore to cram through the hole at all.

He wasn't smooth like a doll but had gone *concave* down there, as whatever awful thing was ravaging him set itself to burrow insatiably through his hips. It was chowing through the fucking *bone!*

'Bring it closer, boy!' With excited grunts and squealings.

To Jack's horror an impossibly long grey tongue slid from the hole, probing for him. Reptilian, and dripping with a clotted straw coloured wetness that tumbled off in steaming strings. They soaked his shoes with a splat, and burned the hell out of his toes.

Finally the spell broke. Screaming mindlessly Jack fled the toilet, utterly heedless of the puzzled students occupying the park who stopped their laps in the downpour and turned to watch him stumble by.

A few of the younger kids burst into tears, sure something terrible had transpired. One or two apple-cheeked team leaders even started toward him with a hand raised, instinctively seeking to help. But Jack's staring eyes were so wild and raw they flinched back.

Wailing, he ran home alone.

No change of heart was going to be Jack's salvation. Even avoiding the third cubicle like the plague, the inexorable progression continued.

Hollowed out. Devoured by a ravenous hole that tunnelled through his body, leading to nowhere and nothing.

His legs became unhinged, rattling loosely in their incomplete sockets, making his gait strange. He took to wearing baggy clothes that flapped about like sails, and then finally padding out his frame to hide the increasing bits that were missing.

A cloth-and-stuffing boy. A rag doll. He employed anything he could filch without his ma finding out: spare cushions, balled-up socks. As Jack feebly wound lengths of bandage about himself to hold it all in place he looked away from the mirror, sobbing and shuddering helplessly with revulsion.

He felt so sad all the time his limbs became to heavy to move, and he fell asleep unpredictably and often. It was his only escape.

The only thing Jack still enjoyed was to sit longingly in the park watching the girls swoop about. As far away from the toilet block as he could get. He only planted himself in full sunlight, wherever a ray could be found. It made him faintly remember happiness, although no amount could make him warm.

Jack sat and wistfully watched the girls jostle in the golden sun. The cut grass smelled so clean. The breeze ruffled his hair. He turned up the hood of his jumper so that no-one could see him weep.

Until one day an ill-aimed football came crashing through the little huddle of clothes. The impact scattered socks and rent cushions, hurling bandages everywhere like an explosion of streamers.

Beth and the girls came tramping over to retrieve their ball, laughing and yelling insincere apologies. But there was nobody at all inside.

THE SELF
MADE MAN

BP GREGORY

THE SELF MADE MAN

THE LITTLE UNSHAVEN bristles of his beard rasped my neck as he breathed. We had argued and then got back to what we seemed best at, and no rubber Johnny in sight if you can believe it.

I had to be out of my sodding mind.

Of the two activities our dispute made a less painful recollection to brood over, where brooding's required.

'So how many tries did it take for me to give over, huh? *How many?* Ten? Twenty? Tell me I at least held out to twenty before dropping with legs in the air, you towering git, give me that much!'

Despite our rough tumble the Timer's regard was neither smeared nor satiated; rather, his face looked eerily bottomless. Eyes like sly lightless wells, a depth you'd drop bonelessly into. Where your waterlogged corpse would never return to light. Cheery.

'What difference does it make?' Was all he had for me.

I threw up my hands with a tone that shrieked and swooped humiliatingly. 'What difference? Are you serious?' Should some inquiring pervert peep through the blinds I'd doubtless resemble any bum-fluff from a dozen free to air programs. But even knowing the limp spectacle, I was skidding along with out of control momentum. 'It makes a great sodding difference to *me*, bucko! You just went ahead and did what you damned Timers always do; stabbing the world's buttons with your playschool fingers ...'

Distain reached new heights. 'You don't have the faintest idea what "we Timers" are. Not the slightest.' As the Timer sneered he sat up and drew the thin linen around him.

Nice move. Now he was covered and my ass left unflatteringly swinging in the wind, but I refused to entertain anything more productive than to raise my chin and attack. 'No? Then you tell me what it's like to get everything you want, the slightest fancy, sooner or later, huh? 'Cause I'm not seeing a whole lot of downside here. It's not *fair*, you get it?'

'Oh, you're concerned with being fair now.'

'People ... *human sodding beings* are only supposed to get one bite at the pie, that single chance, do or die and if you miss, hey, you miss. Happens to the best of us. You deal with it and life goes on, *that's* what makes us human. But not *Timers*, oh no.'

'Since when?' Suddenly those drowning wells opened up, inviting me to sink to the bottom. 'Where's it written we should only get one try? *Makes us human?* Feed that bullshit to some father who's two seconds too late yanking his son outta the road, 'cause of a stupid loose shoelace. Or the surgeon; try the surgeon on his eighteenth straight hour who makes one slip, just a tiny mistake, and so stands there watching the remains of that child drain away. Wanting to be horrified but just thinking numbly *now, finally I can stop.* Do you reckon they'd choke it down as being "fair"?'

The Timer hadn't at all resembled the earthly equivalent of a deity, the closest our dour species was ever likely to get. I suppose its proximity to cleanliness made godliness just as tricky to maintain when wrapped in rented sheets.

No, he had felt like ... a man. That was the long and short of it. And hey, it could be everything, given the right conditions. The only peace there was. His heavily wooded smell rising off him like steam, his warm weight and skin had pushed back the wildly clamouring world for a blessed handful of hours.

I didn't even know his name. Well he had to have one tucked away somewhere: Timers were born and lived like any old jerk, until they flipped and became something ... abnormal. Lacking material I'd instead murmured, '*Timer*,' over and over, the invocation chanted by frightened folk hoping to keep his dread sort at bay. It didn't work for arse, of course. Nothing was going to avail once a Timer set his cap, for he had all the damn time in the world.

I found to my astonishment that the Timer was gentle and skilled and rough and clumsy, like any man. His breath and quick slippery vulnerability were white noise filling up the room and I remembered writhing helplessly beneath him, tiny birdlike noises flying free.

'*Don't go,*' Justin had pleaded frantically, holding my face and staring into my eyes to look for rationality. '*A Timer'll say anything.* And now the funky old sweat and recriminations that wound me about weren't Justin's. All because my stubborn arse wouldn't listen.

No, that wasn't honest. I did listen; and then swanned off on my haughty way, anyhow.

We had been doing our washing at the laundromat, Justin and I. A warm, humming little dump with the dubious honour of being around the corner from our flat, which was all we needed to recommend it.

So far as I could make out the laundromat was overseen by one lemon-faced biddy at least as run down as the building, who'd stare at you like a lizard if you dared ask for change until you got uncomfortable enough to sod off. Delinquents like us were fully expected to smuggle the battered machines away the instant her back was turned and so she wouldn't budge from her corner, not even for a tinkle which had to take some heroically crossed legs.

Speaking of tinkles the entry bell did just that, a fantastically kitsch little clockwork mousie that was *so* this neighbourhood and the only thing I'd genuinely consider stealing. I was stuffing things in the dryer but our charming chaperone glanced up from her *SHOCK NUDE INCREDIBLE BLITZ!* article with *FULL COLOUR PHOTOS!* the incorrigible old perve. Her eyes widened into a pair of round peeled eggs, and the magazine clattered from nerveless fingers to the floor.

Somehow I knew who had come in. Despite having my back to the door, previously engrossed in whatever Justin had to say. I *knew*, even before the prim madam's shocked intake of breath and hurried mumble of *Timer, Timer* that would do sweet fuck-all to keep our visitor away, but it was all she had.

A Timer. The soapy air seemed to thin and lighten, as though he brought his own little glimmer of sunshine.

'So that's what happened to you?' I pressed. 'Botched surgery? Your boy ran into the road?'

'Presumption isn't going to be good for your health. You don't know the least thing about me.'

'No?' I felt pretty au fait with the first, though. I knew the Timer's warm, warm flesh. His faster breathing, coming in little "whuff"s that had sparked a responsive thrill in my gut.

'No. You don't know a fucking thing.'

'Holy carp!' Yes, he said carp; Justin had a thing with swearing. His voice bellowed like a bullhorn in the tiny laundromat and I flinched. 'Keep your voice down!' And his hurt wasn't anything to me, not right now. 'A Timer, I know. What's he doing?' I was too petrified to swing about for a gander myself although not with fear, oh no. Something more sinister ran up from the floor like an electric current, fusing me into place.

Justin briefly treated me to his patented disbelieving sneer: had eyes in the back of my head now, did I? And a dose of quite natural jealousy that when it came to the Timer I'd jumped straight to "he." How had I known?

Acting the spy he obediently snuck a look over my shoulder—we fed off one another's theatrics. And I took the opportunity to study Justin. I could trace all the places he'd end up with wrinkles like gaping canyons one day, especially around the eyes. Made you itch to take an iron to them. Amazement made the roadmap crease like old tortoise skin. 'He's doing his laundry!' Justin pronounced in a throttled stage whisper.

'What?' Decorum fell out the window, I *had* to look.

I spun on the spot and yep, there was the Timer. A man with somewhat endearingly daggy hair. Older than us—perhaps in his late forties, which made me shudder. Thousands of iterations then, depending on when he became a Timer. Or perhaps they were infinite, who knew?

If the fellow hadn't been a Timer he'd have been thoroughly unremarkable, the invisible sort, but there you had it. He *was*. And just as Justin reported, the Timer was indeed doing his own washing. Which didn't make any sense; it blew my tiny mind. I mean, look at him! Carrying his own basket and all!

The proprietress seemed as if she might bolt if she could only persuade her legs to work, livelihood be damned, and I stole the opportunity to wink at her. Never miss a chance to be a witty arse. If looks could kill I'd be roasting.

'What's he up to?' My discretion was of a far better part than Justin's, the Timer couldn't possibly have heard me.

He looked up all the same and smiled. One small, embarrassed moue at himself and the whole ridiculous situation before returning to poking about the washer's panel for a Rosetta stone. I was left with a disquieting impression of those dark eyes, like chill black water. A tide lapping gently at my brain.

I breathed.

The carpet here wasn't much to stare at. That standard downtrodden browny-greeny-bluey-grey of motel furnishings everywhere. A magic shade, that, the colour of economy. The only other place you saw it reproduced was by hyperactive preschoolers, those biting screaming kids who feel the need to combine *all* the paints. The carpet stretched away from the edge of the bed like a vast, arid frontier.

Without turning around I could hear the Timer's resting body. Blood was being industriously shunted through arteries by the steady *whump whump* of his heart. Loud air swooshed in and out of his lungs. Underneath, an active gut muttered about onions. He sounded so ordinary. Like any man. I stared, I listened, and I breathed.

Poor Justin would be back at home right now while we lounged about. Brooding on his own. Cursing me for a bastard and a miserable whore.

He had laughed as the Timer prodded gingerly at the washing machine: the laundromat was our place, after all, we knew all the moves. Something inside me scrunched tight; God, I hated him laughing at other people like that. We all have to put ourselves out there as a noob sometime, otherwise we'd never learn and never progress. But some folk, they just love to kick down. Born perfect, they are.

'Why doesn't he just come back and try again?' Showing off his deep insightful knowledge of Timers. 'Or maybe this is his hundredth time around, and he just can't master beating rags on flat river rocks like the rest of us peasants.'

Now Justin's whiny, aggressive tone was really getting my back up. Like some puny dog: threatened, profoundly threatened by the big bad world, charging pointlessly to the end of his leash until he strangled himself with it. Always yap yap yapping at nothing at all. 'Why don't you show him the way of it then, big man?'

'Why don't *you*?' he shot back, all schoolyard speed, and not to my credit I reacted just as predictably.

'Maybe I will!' My plastic chair groaned back across the tiles.

'Hey, sit your ass down! What the hell do you think you're doing?'

'Relax, Jax.' I brushed myself off … well, I brushed *Justin* off really, wishing that nervous little tingle in my gut would sod off.

'I'll just traipse over, show off my mad peasant laundry moves, and be back here safe and sound. Five minutes, tops.'

Panic surfaced bright and shiny in Justin's stare now it was all going too far. Of course, our afternoon could never be complete without the background whiff of suspicion, and accusation. Just what you get when sticky glands win over brain. Justin sure was your basic glands type. At times like this, poking that bruise could be so gratifying.

He tried to back-pedal, my victory complete. 'Stop! Don't—don't go.'

'So, do you *want* to hear what being a Timer's about, then? Do you really want to know what it's like to hear from yourself *all the time*?'

I did, actually. But that tone begged to differ, so I came over all diffident. Diffident while bare-ass to somebody hogging the sheets was a real art form. 'Every man and his dog knows how you lot cheat. Telling yourself what to do and how to get your own way, all beamed in from the future. You've got the world's best tipping agency.'

'No, you *don't* know! Not even close.' The Timer's superior self control suddenly fractured and he flushed, compressed and angry. 'I'm not "told" anything, there are no tips! That me, from further on down the line, he just *makes* me into the past that he wants, and too bad if I crack when forced into that mould. He makes me walk, he makes me talk, he makes me fucking *breathe* if the way I'm about it isn't to his liking!'

'He … but you mean *yourself*, right? You're talking about your future self. He's *you*.'

'I call him "him" because I'm not that fuckwit yet, not by a long shot. He's my future, up ahead. And he's here, too. I can feel him always tweaking what I do, even now as I'm speaking with you. Correcting mistakes before I get a chance to make them. He's always at me, dirty fingernails picking through my skull, and I hate him! You hear?' Addressing empty air. 'I hate you!'

'But he's *you*,' I repeated. Our conversation had become some nuts carousel whirling 'round and 'round, throwing off sanity and normality like kids flying in all directions. The lights a blur, and tinkling candy floss music become a long scream.

'Can't you get it? I'm not him, not yet. And by the time I become him, he's slipped off to be somebody else. I don't even sleep unless he wants me to, unless he sees some use for it.' The Timer caught his rant visibly, striving for calm. He craved understanding and sympathy as much as the next fellow, but was still too hard and proud to ask. 'Damned puppeteering bastard. I can't get out from under him.'

I rubbed my face, trying to get my head around all this but you'd need your frontal lobes stretched like taffy. 'Aren't you doing exactly the same thing, though? To all the ... the ex-yous?'

'I'm shacked up in my former selves, sure, and they the ones before them. While my tormentors are at the mercy of all those who come after, right down the line. It only travels one way. That's what being a Timer is. As many stabs at the past as you like, but none for the future. A Timer doesn't get a future. So he can put his hands on anything, anything he desires, except peace from himself.'

'But what does that mean for you?' It was too much, I couldn't imagine it. One man spread out to thousands and stacked atop each other like a playing deck. And the wires, the wires to make them dance, that only led down.

'Imagine never being alone inside your own head. And the exhaustion of never being able to stop and enjoy all you've won, not ever. There's only the beat of go, go, go. Do the next thing, change something else.'

'What if he let you go?' It seemed pretty obvious.

The Timer looked at me like I was an idiot, which I suppose I was, and naked to boot. 'He can't. He *won't*. Our past is almost perfect now, so close you can smell it but there's always just one more little nudge. This or that could have been handled better. History is never going to be good enough to merely leave it be.'

The Timer stopped talking. It was rage as well as pain making those midnight wells boil up. A deep breath before continuing. 'I suppose somewhere up ahead just for a second I might be free in that brief instant before I die. When there's no more line, no more me ... I'll bet he's happy, that me who's about to die. He's the happy one. The rest of us can't get there fast enough.'

'Am I meant to feel *sad* for you?' Angry at myself as well, but always far easier to spread it around. 'Oh boo hoo. You chose to be a Timer, if you've forgotten. Nobody twisted your nip.'

'I didn't know what it meant! How could I? All I understood, all I cared about was changing the way I'd lived my life. To make it good enough, to make it *better* ...'

'You've given up your humanity, you have. What could possibly have been so important?'

The Timer laughed hoarsely, a bucket of nails rattling. 'To not have to want anymore. Not ever.'

The bar fridge was humming, complacent and low, a sound to shiver your back teeth loose. It reminded me of a bastard anniversary tradition Justin and I had upheld for many years: liberate everything in your hotel room that's not screwed down. One year he even brought a screwdriver, and I laughed so hard I whizzed a bit.

Justin.

I didn't realise I'd made a sound of protest until the Timer mumbled questioningly, the fingers of one hand exploring the woolly landscape of my thigh. I found it suddenly crushing, unbearable, and finally understood the sound I had wanted to make. 'Stop it.'

'Stop?' The Timer laughed softly. 'Don't you know you can't deny a Timer anything?'

'I mean it.' I slid out from under his pawing, not just off the bed but across the room, folding both arms defensively over my chest. A great gesture when other things were just dangling in the breeze. Trying like hell to keep *plucked turkey* from my mind but the mirror doesn't lie, baby.

His arrogance had tweaked anger awake. 'Why me, huh?' The eternal question, if your ego cools off enough to ask.

The Timer's answer was straightforward and calm. And one hundred percent asshole. 'Because you didn't want me.'

'Huh?'

'Why else do we force anyone to do anything against their will? You, my friend, you were the last straw in a long chain of things denied.'

'*Huh?*'

'Let me tell you a little story, now. I'm sure we've got time. Picture a park. The park's full of the deep greens of summer, the air a thick treacle of heat. There's this invasive pollen smell, unavoidable and full of a blind unstoppable vitality that would charge any normal senses eagerly.

'Yet there stand I. Not a Timer, not yet. Ordinary. No warmth touches this ordinary man's core. With all life in full swing about him he is a throbbing abscess of ice about to burst.

'This absence of heat terrifies our fellow, and he's sick of being afraid. Sick *from* being afraid. There's a bath already drawn in his flaking little flat. In films the liberated redness always tendrils out gracefully through such clear, clean water but the pipes in his building are bung. His bath sits filled with a clotted brown liquid, and it waits patiently for him to come home. However long it will take.

'Unbeknownst to anyone, the extremity of this fellow's anguish has drifted outside the sphere allocated to ordinary beings. Straying into the real that drives artists to paint laughing with brushes of their own sinew and bone. Already he is on the road to becoming something else.

'All this running through his fool head like some icy underground river. Now imagine he suddenly notices a man in that park. A lovely man. So lovely. Seated peacefully on a bench, not hurting anybody, just enjoying the air.'

'Man, spotted in his natural habitat. Grazing on twigs, leaves and cigarette butts.' My attempt at levity only darkened the atmosphere further. What the Timer radiated sent a shiver of dread through me, although I guessed if I wanted out he'd have a hard time preventing me flying through the door to run that corridor, starkers, all the way home. Waves of invisible snow streamed off him, straight from the winter of the midnight sun. A wind that would strip flesh from bone.

'He began to walk toward this other person in the park. Mechanically, like a puppet, because everything he did was ugly. Approaching from behind he could stare all he liked. The lovely stranger had short blond hair that swept the base of a squarish neck. His shirt stuck to his back. He knew, somehow, how this man would smell in the heat: male sweat, healthy as a horse, under a strong mask of deodorant. Something with cloves.

'It used to be *me* who wanted,' the Timer croaked, and the icy gale blew harder. 'Me who got nothing. Every day the wretched wanting of what others had, so pathetically jealous of everyone on the street and so *angry* …'

No doubts on that last one: his eyes were ugly with it, piteous and enraged. His big mitts clenched white by his sides as though he'd shake me for my inability to get with the program.

Fling a rag doll around until he heard the sickening crunch of vertebrae. Had he killed me before? Already, in this very hotel room, a million times, a million Timers?

'How the hell could someone like you understand? How could you possibly know what it's like to really *want*, with a face like that?'

The Timer never asked, but I could recite quite the tale of my own, you see. About dazedly entering a cheap nasty hotel with no idea of how being at the laundromat had led to here. The Timer's influence yanking me about until I could hardly tell what was here and now. Could I be remembering the past? Or was it rushing mell pell toward me from the future, echo preceding cause, some insane Doppler effect of reality?

The Timer said something I could not hear, triumphant and boastful, just trawling for a smack. He was somewhere behind me now; just as he must have stood behind that park bench with covetous eyes drilling into my neck. I heard a door click shut although I couldn't remember booking the room. It was dark in here, the blinds closed ranks and I trembled in the sudden intimacy of the space.

He said it again, hot breath against my neck. I could smell what he'd wolfed down for lunch as clearly as though I'd eaten it myself. He was hesitant to touch me. At first.

Yep, I could have recounted a little tale if he'd cared to hear, all about curiosity twisting the cat. But other people's stories were never as good as your own.

Outside, airbrakes hissed. Bright spangles kicked off chrome, slipped right through the blinds and invaded our room as the truck swept by. Shadows and light raced briefly along my body and the Timer's face as though chasing one another. The marks of his overeager mouth were splashed down my throat, and how would I explain that to Justin's crumpling face? My shit might well be on fire in the street when I got home, and fair enough.

However, it was the illumination of the Timer that captivated. He dipped his face to hide behind a stringy fringe and sniffed wetly. I stood and watched him cry.

In the awkward silence the humming fridge clicked and above it a spider was scaling the wall on legs like needles. The Timer sat in a lump on the bed, all pointed corners I could grind to pieces on and I wanted to move further away across a room that had nowhere to go. Instead I returned and sat behind him. I ran one hand across his shoulders: tactile, I could feel him, which to me made this the solid here and now. But could *he* hear *me* through the tumult in his head? 'Timer.'

A choked sound from him. 'There, in that park I stood behind you and eventually you turned your head a little. The motion dislodged this tiny bead of sweat that spiralled 'round the curve of your neck like some joyous candy cane stripe. My guts convulsed when your eye skittered over me, I thought I'd be sick. I could see myself in you, reflected back. Too late you pretended to be studying the trees behind me.

'Piping hot rage was the first real emotion to happen along for ages and I was totally unprepared. How *dare* you despise me like that, the merest sight, without even *knowing* me! You just dismissed me right out of reality!

'I wrestled my advance to a halt before my shadow fell on you, close enough to spy tiny wisps of blond that curled and stuck in the moisture at the nape of your neck. I wanted to slick them down with my mouth. I wanted to rip them out.

'Hate is wonderful for personal change. The rage catalysed as nothing else could. Standing there, struggling not to move I felt another self push within my skull for the first time, with dreadful clarity. A monstrous domineering presence I recognised all too well and finally, finally I understood what I had become.

'And I smiled at the back of your neck. The relief that sagged your shoulders as I backed away was a magnificent insult to injury, but I merely smiled. I'd make you come to me—crawling maybe, who knows? That's how everything would be from now on.'

'Timer,' I said again; he was a title, not a name. My body knew him so well. Knew his feel and smell as though a ghost still resided in me. If I licked my lips I'd taste him. The Timer shuddered beneath my touch like a machine about to fly apart and I loved the power of it, as I always had.

'Timer. You need to let them go. All of them.' His eyes flashed to my face and though my insides quailed I didn't duck, no more than you'd back down from a dangerous dog. They said you couldn't deny a Timer, but I had always been handed the world on a plate, never lifting a finger, like all of life's rare blessed. Who knew what I could accomplish by trying?

You see, I'd fancied taste testing a Timer for a long time. But this little jaunt had gone far enough. 'Don't you understand? They're at different stages, sure, but those men are still you. It only takes one of you to give up power for all to follow. If you release your stranglehold, so will they.' If he let go, his bath of clotted slime would still be waiting.

A surge seemed to pass though the Timer and he visibly tensed in on himself like a fist. I breathed. I waited.

'Yes.' His answer was: 'Yes.'

Justin and I walked into the laundromat, holding hands. The sky overhead was blue, overripe with vitality, glorious. It was going to be a beautiful day.

A SHORT STORY

Submerged
BP GREGORY

SUBMERGED

THE HALL FLOOR was no place for an old bastard; but as painfully cramped as the contortion was Brendan remained huddled pathetically below the peephole. Fierce shudders flung off hectic sweat in spatters before it could run into his eyes. And hey, with his hammering heart fixing to thrash its way free perhaps he'd never make it up off the crinkly carpet at all—wouldn't that be something?

A long time since his corpus ceased being a neglected convenience; by now the damned thing had regressed to a positive hindrance. Luckily the world came pretty much delivered these days, about the best you could say for it. Chuck in a fiver to get it lugged up the stairs he could no longer manage.

So far as Brendan saw, the only dreadful thing about being marooned in his apartment lay right across the way: his brightly-smiling neighbours who'd just graduated in a flash from mere troubling to downright terrifying. Straight to the head of the class.

At first he'd merely despised them cordially, same as any starstruck couple gazing into one another's eyes. You could see how they formed their own staunch dyke against the world, raw salt in the wound of what Brendan still missed every damn day.

Then came the disturbances.

It was the only possible term, they were so very bloody disturbing, and also incredibly faint. Tenuous enough to convince yourself, after a bit of a rational think, that your florid imagination must have run off. Brendan figured you would have to be a sour, isolated old goat stranded in a dead-quiet apartment to even hear what mindless desperation scritched at the plaster.

Next, the dank tendrils of water that seeped under the crack of their door to discolour the landing.

Brendan had always hated water. Maybe it was the long skinny shanks, but he couldn't float: without constant exhausting effort it was straight to the bottom and stay there. Damn near drowned on a youth camp before the lifeguard quit ogling pre-teens long enough to figure out that the gangly youth wasn't fooling.

Having survived the Disaster Brendan limited his exposure to scrubbing his drooping flesh with a cloth at the sink, the shower bone dry. A wash time spectacle of his pallid backside hanging out that would have had Joyita in stitches; although she wouldn't have put up with an iota of his crazy old bugger nonsense in the first place.

Smelling not quite right, like a tub where you'd cleaned fish but left the scaly jelly to stand for days, the intrusion had lurked innocently beneath the landing carpet ... until it came squishing and slobbering in through Brendan's socks.

He'd not been thinking further than fresh coffee and toast and the bolt of brutal chill up his old legs was such an awful surprise that he half-fell against the wall, hissing shrilly as though scalded.

A flood—well that wasn't unnatural in itself, however one feels about water. These things happen. But even as the reclusive neighbours replaced his groceries that had sat out in it and got foul they were beaming. Big toothy canine grins that suggested *sorry* was furthest from the truth.

Wet red smiles that spoke without speaking, leered: *hello food*, as they savoured his distress. Shuddering with loathing Brendan hurled his socks in the trash like limp dead animals and always wore shoes after that. He'd loved plodding around in his socks.

Once in the wee hours he'd jolted awake to what he tremblingly swore was a cat shrieking in that agonised feline jet-engine register. Long gone by the time he knocked over his lamp and hyperventilated his way to clicking it on as it lay on the floor, but the echoes guaranteed no more shut-eye, pills or no pills. Perhaps ever.

The jet engines had been screaming. The plane going down disintegrated into a mass of shrieking noise. Even after Brendan's eardrums were repaired so he could at least hear his own anguished sobbing, tucked safe in a hospital bed, he only understood the Disaster as a shattering cacophony.

He certainly hadn't bloody well wanted to get out of the fuselage into the water. Let him go down with the plane! Somebody ought to. It was a good plane; it'd got them … most of the way.

Joyita had known how to manage him. A fellow came to lean on certainty like that.

They told amused family friends he'd tried to save her from a film shoot, when it was really the other way around. This was a woman who charged straight in and Brendan's "assailant" had found himself face-down with her knee on his spine before he knew what was happening. Only then did Joyita finally notice the camera.

At her chagrined smile Brendan fell instantly and so hard everyone there saw it, even the lass he was dating at the time which was a real shame.

Not that the face-saving white lie of how he met his wife amounted to much now. All those family friends were long gone.

Partially submerged now, the engines had screamed as he jittered from foot to foot. A racket to blow all clear thought from your mind, tumbling helplessly through the air. And from the ocean Joyita coyly extended her arms to Brendan like a siren, beckoning him down into that icy rank-smelling water that clogged his sinuses unbearably even from up here.

Come on honey. Get those chicken-legs in here.

Joyita's canola-bright silk blouse that he loved so much, because she scorned its inane cheer and only ever wore it for him, was a drenched ruin that outlined his wife's chest most becomingly.

I'll float you. Just like in that spa on our honeymoon.

Bless her for remembering a time like that at a time like this. Closing his eyes Brendan had plunged in obediently.

The cold seemed to slap the life right out of him. The fumes were blinding and he was slipping under no matter how desperately he flailed …

Then Joyita's warm strong arms closed firmly about him. She floated him, tilted back in the water on the buoyancy of her own body.

I've got you love.

As the creepiness escalated, at least the burning envy of his neighbours had withered. Even tolerating them in the same apartment block seemed a ripe perversion of what he'd hoped to have. *Brendan and Joyita* were supposed to grow rickety here together, and help each other up the alpine height of the stairs. Instead their home was an empty space where silence rang, and he sat alone and oppressed listening to scratching in the walls.

Now things had suddenly become infinitely worse than simply enduring loneliness for the rest of his days, and Brendan scrabbled a bit at the carpet beneath him in a panic. He was alone, and he didn't know what to do. Not after witnessing what the damn neighbours had just humped up the stairs.

An abduction nightmare. A figure gruesomely swaddled and taped tight in black garbage bags. That thick, slippery type of plastic that nobody splashes out on unless they have some serious repugnance to contain.

It lay gleaming on the landing at their feet as they struggled with their door. Tottering drunk, both of them. Busy stifling inappropriate titters and kissing one another in long drawn out gasps.

The cringing mind frantically longed to dismiss the apparition as a special effect, to restore what sanity had dominated scarce moments before. But even through the tunnel vision of the peephole Brendan's horrified eye could spy movement.

In periodic heaving bellows the cocoon was sucked concave into that bound mouth by struggling lungs. Heavy plastic, black and shiny as ink, vacuum-formed down over the twisted features with each desperate attempt at a breath.

The labour of levering himself from the floor and up the wall felt almost impossible. Come on man, you can do it! The best he could manage once upright—finally! —was to cling to the door handle and patter rank sweat all over the carpet.

Brendan couldn't honestly claim to be afraid of being shot of it all. Not like he'd quivered when the blank, black water had lapped all around, and he could feel warm life abandoning him into the searing air one breath at a time.

The sheer intensity of *that* fear had blown out his emotions, never to recover. Most of what got left inside, as he discovered in the hospital, were merely blackened charred smears. That, and the fading memories of vivid feeling.

What shall we do together?

Joyita's voice had come suddenly from the dark as they floated in the shattering cold. Her arms alone contained the involuntary trembling and jerking of his limbs. Following the sinking of the screaming plane they weren't even left with the distant stars for comfort.

Tell me all the things we're going to do, love. Our whole life. Don't leave anything out.

Oh his cunning Joyita, keeping their minds off things.

So through chattering teeth, he did. With the fond curve of her lips against his chill ear Brendan told her everything and he left nothing out.

Breakfast together every morning. The indulgent holidays they'd scrimp for, pouring over glossy brochures. He knew exactly what he'd buy her for every anniversary, which earned the warm gust of her laughter against his cheek. And they should go dancing—hey, honey, should we take a dance class? Are you listening?

Ssh now. I see a light, love. Do you see a light?

Their rescuers, plying a bright searchlight over the water as they toiled through the frozen night. To whom Brendan had cried out hoarsely with icy tears of joy running down his face.

Unable to hear his own voice, but guiding them in.

Only to be shrieking and writhing to escape moments later. The dinghy was already low in the water with hypothermic survivors stolen from the ocean. They wouldn't take Joyita, indicating to Brendan with sympathetic but impatient signs that she'd been dead many hours.

Against his will he was dragged from the salvation of her arms and over the gunwale, blinded by the searchlight beam as he twisted back and reached with all his feeble might to pull Joyita from the water. The last he saw of his wife was her beautiful smile shining above that yellow blouse he made her wear, as the depths took her.

Brendan didn't know how to banish the monsters next door, but bold Joyita sure would. He could hardly do less.

Almost of its own accord his quivering hand jerked the door open and he was charging onto the landing, a liberated burst of old-man smell freed from his hallway. Rather comically, considering what he faced, coming at them in his determination like an out of control tortoise.

The neighbours had at least managed to unlatch their door before succumbing to a tipsy embrace straight from the rushes of a D-grade porn flick. It would never have worked if they weren't already so off kilter. The woman's startled eyes popped up over her partner's shoulder before Brendan's charge flung the two of them headlong into their own apartment.

Brendan dropped to his knees with an agonised grunt, damn sure he wasn't getting up this time; and tore at the seal over the captive's mouth with his blunt yellow nails. His inflexible gnarled fingers were little better than claws at the task: they skittered and slipped.

Then the wrapped figure inhaled. Cerements sealed to its agonised face and with a jab of the thumb he was able to puncture through to the wet mouth beyond, which with a sob immediately hoovered in air almost hard enough to swallow his hand to the damn elbow.

'Please don't kill me!' the liberated voice hissed through the ragged hole, almost inaudible on a fountain of frothy spit. 'Please. I don't want to leave my kid all by herself.'

This was somebody who'd already come to the extreme of themselves. In that Brendan recognised a brotherhood, one of facing what was left with life taken away. Now even more than when it was just another human being, he quaked with the desire to save the captive if he could.

Then the neighbours were on him. Bouncing back to their feet like a pair of those awful clown dolls, wide grins painted on their faces. So much for his heroism. Brendan was frail, in a faulty body grinding down in multiplying errors to the end of its life. If they'd clonked him on the head like in a movie it might well have killed him.

But no, like housecats they wanted their nasty fun. One on either side, his neighbours' avid greedy fingers yanked him into their apartment.

All of the blinds were drawn. A mass of pain from his wild exertions, Brendan was dragged down a hall which was a mirrored reverse of his own and through a lounge that wavered like a disturbing underwater sort of world, his limbs waving feebly as though swimming. Not even a few cold stars overhead for comfort.

Furniture was little more than a series of looming monoliths in the dimness until he or one of his assailants whacked into it, drawing whimpers from Brendan and muffled snickers from them. They were having a marvellous time. Unable to free itself or encompass the proceedings, his mind vainly tried to go away somewhere. Perhaps to that golden paradise before the Disaster.

But reality had no truck with nostalgia. Dropped with cruel indifference onto cold hard tile Brendan howled as with a crack, sickly heat and agony bloomed in the spindly arm that caught his weight. He rocked back and forth—was the damn thing broken?

One of the neighbours, he couldn't even tell them apart now with their leering wide-open mouths and drooping insatiable eyes, went out; presumably retrieving their other gift-wrapped treat.

The one he was left with loomed overhead and flicked on a light so cold and harsh and startlingly clinical that Brendan cried out again, trying to hide his face in the crook of his good arm. That unforgiving light: This is a place where we dissect people. Right down to the bone.

He was in their bathroom.

Stark tile all around, bluish now in that hard cold light. White towels lined up neatly on a steel rail with surgical precision. Aside from Brendan himself cowering on the floor the only spots of warm colour were a blue and a yellow toothbrush, nestled together in a chipped waterglass on the sink. In his pain and confusion he gaped dumbly up at them, boggling at the ordinariness they advertised.

Oh, it wasn't fair! It was supposed to be *their* worn out toothbrushes propping each other up, his and Joyita's. Everyday implements to be used in tandem as they stood yawning side-by-side at the sink, each morning and before turning in. Socks on in winter, to save their feet from the cold.

A rough hand on his collar dragged him forward. And now he was whining and squealing almost mindlessly, finally comprehending, his legs shuddering and jerking beneath him. Because his neighbours had run the bath for their intended guest. But it would do for him just as well.

Brendan's weeping whiskered face was thrust down into the cold water. His arms threshed and squeaked off porcelain both inside the tub and out, throwing up great sheets of liquid but this wasn't his tormentor's first time: there was no purchase to be had. And even should he dig in, somehow, Brendan was weak. A fool who rushed in. While the hand holding him down by the saggy scruff of his neck was calculatedly strong: too strong, steely and without pity.

Had he thought mortal terror dead? Foolish! Here it waited for him again, his departed friend. The old man felt himself coming unmoored with it and what you could generously call his struggles weakened further.

With an influx of the cold, cold water rushing inside, his overburdened chest clenched and writhed once. Then a second time, wiping all that he cherished away.

Barely there anymore, Brendan was no more than the last tiny star high above in a frozen sky when strong hands closed about him from behind. Warm arms pulling him backward.

These had to be new hands: far from callous, they laid him out on the tile with unbelievable tenderness and trembling anxiety. The squeak of plastic bags torn to shreds but still clinging on. Brendan smiled tremulously even though he couldn't see. All was dark, and though the hands meant well how could he possibly be taken back from the ocean now?

A voice was babbling, panting and almost hysteric in its stumbling outflow, as well it might be. 'Come on old fella, I've got you. Oh come on, please *breathe*! We're gonna be ok— those nutbars weren't banking on two of us, turns out one alone couldn't manage me. I clocked the lass out cold and then rushed in here and did for the guy holding you under.'

A trembling sniff. 'Chucked a book through the window on the way and screamed at an old duck walking the pavement to call the police. If it weren't for you I'd be … Just hold on, the cops'll be here soon—I can see lights coming up the street …'

I see a light!

Not the flickering red and blue of emergency services but a warm cheery yellow rising out of the dark to greet him. And above it, a smile of such sweetness as to stop your heart.

Oh, I see a light.

The tiles were cold against Brendan's cheek and he sighed and closed his eyes, exhausted, in a puddle of his own tears.

I'm so sorry I made you wear that blouse. Take me with you, love. Nothing's ever been nice without you.

And he sank away.

STOW

A short story

STOW

I WAS QUAKING WITH such insane frustration the day they canned the space program that instead of assembling an economical dinner like a good little wifey, I stomped away into the sunset. Off to find where the man had fallen from the sky.

It was weird because I hadn't braved that crumbling old neighbourhood in decades. Nary a flicker of nostalgia either for the treasured bogey of my childhood, that poor fellow who'd flown like a stone. But I found I had to do *something* before my confounded head blew apart.

All adult coping strategies having stripped gears long ago, that left only one force on the good green earth capable of driving such static from my skull, hopefully right off into the sea. A redoubt I must have known I'd return to someday because here I was locking the front door and sliding into the sedan, hands a tremble with anticipation.

I remembered the ritual.

Plant your ass right where the man fell, whispered local legend, leeringly. If you're game, that is. You'll go through all he endured in his final moments, the man who fell from the sky. Like it was saved in a bottle just for you.

With peak hour ebbing the drive took nowhere near as long as I'd imagined. An unwelcome surprise, like I'd zipped across town a hundred times to this suburb, dilapidated since my childhood but that's what you get. Well, hey; bright sarcasm popped up as I banked around long curves, a maze of streets to get lost in. Sure haven't managed to trundle far in one lifetime, have we?

It was a realisation that seasoned bitterness with gall. As I switched off the shuddering engine and climbed from my car I glanced balefully up at a sky ripening to rich purple. No beauty would appease. Not today. Rather, I wished fiercely for a world without a universe, stripped of the sun and shyly unveiling stars because we didn't deserve them. We'd turned our stupid backs on wonder.

And I know what anyone would claim but this was amplitudes worse than when they banned airplanes a few years back, sewing up the sky for birds. I'd gone along with that; perhaps as meekly as any sheep conditioned to flinch from slavering shadows. But what could they possibly claim to be in dread of now? *Space* terrorists?

Most folk were happy as clams with the official line—ooh, they're keeping us safe, let's go shopping. I only supposed any different because once upon a time I'd had a friend. A good friend, a crazy-as-arse friend, and he built a contraband airplane in his garage.

It was something amazing, I'll admit now. A miracle knocked together from industry offcuts and who knows what else. He wanted the clouds; but the mere idea made me all tight and scared inside so I mocked him, to my eternal regret. Went on with my boring life instead.

While my crazy, good friend also became a man who fell from the sky. With a heart, I'd imagine, just as frantic for liberty.

SPACE PROGRAM CANCELLED. Pasting the article between the yellowing leaves of my scrapbook, to be inhaling its comforting must, felt like my end. The road stops here. I mean, scads of starry-eyed lasses yearn just as hard to become astronauts; more than enough for silly old me to grit my teeth and accept, well, we can't all get there.

When I'd started my collection, with pencil grasped firmly in stubby childish fingers for sketching rocketships, only allowed safe scissors and for heaven's sake keep that glue off the carpet, it had seemed to represent all the radiant possibility out there. Horizons that had shut down over time, one by one. Now brittle and gazing mournfully back at me from the page.

I ought to have taken it on the chin: desolation wasn't entirely new territory. First had been my airplane-builder, around the traps so long that his loss left a hollow inflexible void. Quite like when whirring insects shed their carapace outside your window during sticky weather. They creep off to better climes leaving a mere outline clinging awkwardly to the tree, still trying to pretend everything's normal inside.

Two further handfuls of guts scooped out the afternoon my kids sauntered off to Europe. No holiday jaunt in this day and age, not without airplanes. Something of a trap, too, from what I've heard. You step off the boat with dusty pockets and must work and work and work. Scrabble to marry ends so reluctant to meet, and good luck ever affording another ticket. Reasonable then to assume that my babies, off over the skyline, would never return.

They'd both known it, too. Even as they pressed a dry kiss to my sallow cheek, one either side, with a blithe *Be home before you know it, Mum. Be seeing you again.* Tripping smartly up the gangplank while I'd clutched my elbows against the dock's garbage-brine miasma instead of waving, practically levitating so as not to touch anything. A crumpled old kerchief over my hair like the worst kind of war bride.

Cross sections of old scar tissue, those void spots within. Nevermore to change or evolve. And as more and more folk up and abandoned my life, I was becoming mummified by it.

I waited at the car for a bit as the last light fled, listening to the world creak and settle in. Chewing grim thoughts. It became chilly, and a feverish infant in the distance twisted my heart as its wail echoed on and on down that depressing, dark street. No cheery lamps comforted this neck of the woods, not anymore, although I'd no compunctions back in the day as a wee nip to go slithering out my window.

As a matter of fact, I knew that the cracked bit of pavement up there was really just where *most* of the man who'd fallen ended up. An impact like that wasn't conducive to a whole body, even one iced solid. A few centimetres left or right and it would have been a freshly mown lawn receiving tribute, or a lovely white picket fence. Folk cared about their yard back then, they seemed to have time to. One of the few titbits retained from a blurry childhood of scissors and glue: how nice everything looked.

For a few days the body had become a minor celebrity where it lay smashed on the ground. The sweltering heat rose and glassy ice slowly melted down to a little pool with the tragedy of a dropped icypole.

In spite of what advanced into a jellifying stench folk came to poke their beaks into this mystery the dawn had revealed. It was lazy summer holidays, they'd time to burn. First from other, envious streets whose footpaths remained pristine. Then they were traipsing from right the other end of town.

Eventually, *tourists.*

Real crowds of folks, some of whom I didn't even recognise. Shoving each other and giggling, real unruly. Daring in brash voices for you or *you* to be first. Sneak in close enough to be in on that much vaunted final, mortal sensation. You'd think it a carnival ride.

Even the inevitable result repeated again and again only slapped fuel on rumour. The bravest souls were rewarded with blanching and cruel shakes head to toe for all their daring; snickering silenced. They hurried away from fuss and friend shaking their heads like they wanted to be sick.

Then the bomb dropped, so to speak.

The authorities, the police, *someone* determined that the man had been a stowaway, nothing more. Dropped like fluttering trash from a passing airliner when the landing gear extended. In fact his shoe, torn off and left behind, jammed a piston and almost triggered a catastrophe—lucky you can't arrest a corpse.

Deceased. Either frozen, or crushed whimpering in the dark, perhaps suffocated cyanotic blue. There were dozens of ways to die such a tawdry death. Perhaps this poor fellow had endured them all.

Public interest tapered off sharply. The crowds turned way with a genteel sort of embarrassment: it was unseemly to desire more, to hope a different life might be better. The man who'd fallen from the sky was duly left to sink into the pavement, beaten flat by the sun and only occasionally by rain. To deal with the mess, well now, that would have meant acknowledging it.

Even at such a tender thoughtless age it had boggled my mind how he lay there, day in and day out, and no-one came for him. *Nobody.* Had they the means? Presumably he'd set out from someplace poor, poorer than this, and terribly far away. Could his family not know how he'd ended up here among green lawns and clicking sprinklers, and folk bound up in their own problems who looked real hard the other way?

It was noted, yet not noted, that no animals scavenged those pitifully exposed remains. Beasties seemed to sense something radiating off him, just as the tourists had, and they didn't fancy it one bit. Ants sometimes meandered onto the corpse and died for no reason, as if in sympathy, curled up like little black crumbs. Mother Nature had zero interest in helping.

I *did* once see the crossing guard's puffball Pomeranian try for a thighbone. It was a ridiculous prospect: the mutt could hardly have lifted it. But as a numbskull, little Roxie stood tall amidst a breed not notable in the brains department.

The moment her puny jaws touched bone she recoiled, and went streaking away up the street crying blue murder. Right by my bike, and I felt her passage as a horribly cold breeze against my leg. It was but a glimpse, mind, but crackling frost had glittered on the poor mite's circus-orange fur.

It was no sight for a kid, to witness saggy flesh liquefying from splintered bone as summer progressed. Indelibly staining the pavement beneath. Not an enjoyable view for anyone, as the sprouting thicket of SALE signs attested.

Awareness that in this day and age one should be driven to such an end, to in fact have your nose rubbed in it, gradually poisoned off the happiness of the formerly peaceful suburb. It was impossible to unwind after work confronted by something like that, you could only crank tighter. And it was hardly ok to invite the neighbours around for a barbeque.

My mother was facing a losing battle, especially after the thing with the dog: try telling any kid to keep away from anything. For the record, I'd hardly succeeded in keeping the glue off the carpet either; my bedroom was crunchy underfoot, the topic of many a tanned backside. When I had my own rugrats I let them merrily sketch and paste the house down, and even so many years later it felt like sweet sodding revenge.

Anyway, I think I made up some story in my head that the man had secretly dropped all the way from space. My peers were all idiots and jerks for buying that airplane guff, nobody'd be crazy enough to cram themselves into the frigid oily darkness of a wheelwell. I'd peered behind the car's tyres to get an idea of what it was like, and shuddered at the filthy pocket.

The urge to sneak out one night and visit him, my secret astronaut, became irresistible. He had a message for me.

I'm not positive what others experienced, stepping from a neatly shorn patch of grass into the murk, the stink. The creaking of busy insects stopped—everything stopped. From the stifling summer night, it was like being pushed into a pool when you're not ready. Plunging into breath stopping frigid water. My skin cringed three sizes smaller.

What I felt was desperation.

I tasted the sheer, trapped panic of a life you would do anything, at any cost, to escape. Nothing in my brief, comfortable existence married up with it and with a profound loss I understood that, truly, he was no astronaut. Just a man in an impossible situation. Of course he climbed right into that terrible wheelwell, with eyes wide open. He would have done anything.

I stumbled backward onto the grass. All bruised up inside where nobody could kiss it better. Profoundly weak in every chill joint, as from a long season battling the mumps. The warm night flooded back in, thick air you could scarcely draw, cicadas singing to the stars.

And I felt unexpectedly, astonishingly alive.

Like an addict I had to go back for it, again and again. It consumed my nights and I became a dull eyed, exhausted child, peering through a curtain of lank hair. The sort of child nobody can love. My grades tanked, weight ballooned and reflexes degraded so badly that the postal truck veered within whiskers of cleaning me right off my bike.

All I'd been able to manage was to stare numbly at the driver, him hallooing out the window and shaking his fist to raise the dead. After a moment he seemed to realise that something was very wrong. Instead of serving my parents a piece of his mind he drove off rather quickly, an uncomfortable look on his face.

But, ah, my secret scrapbook flourished. Children invest such vivid power in little bods and rituals. Unfortunately, what's healthy for an imaginative youth becomes less so to the adult struggling to make sense of their world.

No summer stretches its lazy paws out forever, and eventually my parents scraped together the resource to follow our neighbours. We moved away. I'm pretty sure Mum and Dad lost a packet on the glue caked house, each grim decision made worse by me screaming and sobbing every step of it.

I could no longer visit the midnight pavement. But as it turned out I was still venturing *somewhere* when night fell, a habit that couldn't be broken. Sleepwalking, I guess. It wasn't nice waking with my nightgown inside-out, muck between my toes. Sometimes I'd be clutching something ice-cold for dear life, as though terrified I'd let go and fall. Something that sucked the heat straight down my arm. A thing I'd toss in the trash with a shudder without flicking the light on to see.

Mysterious. Implacable. My husband didn't have an inkling of it until matters became recently worse. Bless his stoic, ordinary heart, he suspects I've taken some kind of lover. I can't pin him down long enough to illuminate just how laughable that is: I don't even have any friends. Only work acquaintances I can't wait to escape, who gabble in the foreign language of TV shows and gossip.

I only had that one friend. Funnily enough, he'd been the first to red flag that all wasn't well when I went to bed of a night.

Wish I'd listened to him instead of toodling along, digging myself in deeper—and how he'd smirk to hear me confess as much. If he hadn't plummeted flaming from the forbidden heavens in the most outlandish way possible.

The man who'd fallen from the sky, ice rather than fire, was gone now. Only a faint shadow remained at my toes, although I'd know this skerrick of pavement anywhere.

On the brink of stepping aboard I hesitated, astounding myself. Wasn't this what I wanted? I was practically all alone these days. Really, what was the worst that could happen?

My breath plumed in the unfriendly air. I gaped at the sudden, jarring realisation that nothing was keeping me here. Or any place.

Perhaps that's why I wandered instead of staying safely abed when the stricter parts of my brain shut down. I was trying to tell the waking me that it was possible, entirely possible to just walk right out of this life I had built. To go eagerly to that sense of promise that awaited, somewhere over the horizon. If I only stopped resisting.

I had been too vividly feeling all of my friend's fear, and my husband's suspicion, but nothing for myself. I too, after a fashion, was being called to stow away. To let something infinitely vaster than myself, something inexorable carry me to some unknown destination, that had to be better than this.

Unseen in the darkness, a crooked smile limped across my face at the prospect, muscles stiff from disuse. Perhaps ... I could make it all the way to the stars.

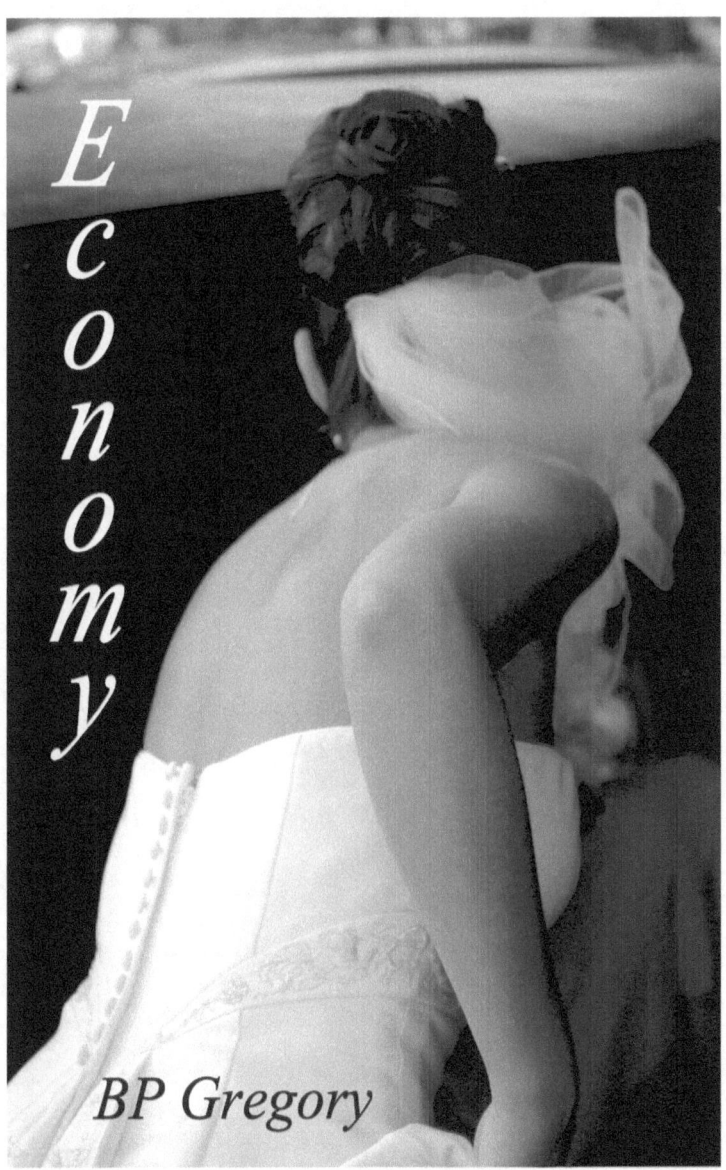

Economy

BP Gregory

ECONOMY

THESE ECONOMY MODELS sure were cheap as newly minted ass to run, you couldn't fault them that. Just feed in whatever rag-tag scraps of yourself you weren't using, scads of juicy fat to be trimmed 'round the edge of the average workaday, and you were hot to trot. Essentially the car ran on emotion, sucked it up like a sponge. And in those stakes Babette was blazing hot enough to melt a hole right through it.

But damn the wheels were sluggish out of the gate. Wandering all over the road like a somnambulist in the face of Babette's urgent need to fly, and she cursed herself wild for having fallen for the safe bet. Yet again.

Oh, apple green on twinkling chrome had looked so cheerful—well now she bloody knew, didn't she. The sodding thing smelled dead. A dry, rental upholstery must blew through the vents like halitosis, loaded with the harsh chems used in embalming whatever made it tick. Fake vanilla on top that coated her gums with every inhale, sickly icing managed to conceal the deadness until she had driven far, far from the lot.

She fed it her revulsion. Plenty of that to share around and served the damn thing right. Although of all the gross oddities the car seemed to *like* slurping nausea down like a milkshake, giving a brief kick of the heels up to eighty. For her part Babette sat forward, a good few kilograms lighter without that constant urge to hurl her cookies. The seatbelt clicked in tighter, taking up the slack.

Huh. A harried glance at her beaten down old watch, sweeping the alchemy of automotives aside for now. It was ten o'clock already. The wedding was due to kick off at twelve.

Hammering the wheel Babette cursed out her lousy pittance job for withholding the raises year after year that would've let her buy a proper car. Never mind all her labour to haul their sodding business out of the dark ages, oh no, always the same sour old tune no matter who hummed along.

Gathered unto themselves with both grasping hands, they did. Beaming delightedly the greedy world took and took. Oh *Babette*, you're so *nice*. Lauded qualities she could tick off on her fingers: unfailingly kind, cloyingly sweet; the French polish snapping away like gunfire. A regular Mother Teresa.

What had "nice" ever garnered, other than straight to the bottom of the heap? Well not anymore, boyo. Not this time.

Speaking of which she risked another paranoid peek at the time, a manoeuvre becoming tricksy as she accelerated. Ah. Eleven now. Earlybird guests would be poking desultorily around the church grounds, yawning fit to crack and wishing for a coffee to sand the edges off.

Sure as shit through a goose Babette wasn't travelling fast enough to make the ceremony, even with her foot flat to the floor and calf singing falsetto, so she crammed all of her carefully hoarded resentment down the car's smacking maw. Every last drop. Leaving her bobbling about, airy and insubstantial, deep breaths just to stay rooted to the here-and-now.

No profit in holding onto that sourness anymore, anyhow. Not since Dave had encouraged her to strike out. *Discover who you've always wanted to be, baby.* Like such revelations came naturally to anyone bold enough to step from the line.

Only, coming from his smiling mouth, quirked with kindness, she'd finally believed and wasn't that something. It was like ... being let out of a box. Somebody taking the lid off and letting in air, and all this time you'd thought it was *supposed* to be dark.

Oh God. Dave.

A glimpse in the rearview confirmed her peepers were still scratchy and raw as though she'd industriously scrubbed lemon into each. Too many nights brooding on the ideal birthday gift she'd had on lay-by, their stillborn planned road trip together, and all those swank restaurants she'd never dare show her face in now. Not alone.

I'm going through with it, Dave had confessed in bed, in sodding bed! It ought to be *her* wedding. *Her* "perfect day;" a concept never dreamed of as a snotty tomboy, that'd left her cold and bewildered through her teens, but which sprang full into life the very instant she met Dave. Pumping its fist and screaming about white lace.

Fat lot of good all this hazy nostalgia would accomplish if she didn't beat "Do you?" to the punch line, so she sieved her giddy romanticism into the car too, wincing when it greedily sucked her fingers. Reeled in her seat. Faint. Having difficulty even seeing the road, until her vision steadied on the scratched watch face.

Eleven thirty.

Come on, come on. She clamped down on herself with a rigid will. The engine whirred.

It was all Babette could manage to fend off visions of those merrymakers crammed into the chapel. Mouths behind shocked hands when she came bursting in, out of breath and sweaty. She had so carefully never allowed herself to learn the blushing bride's name, but the horror on the poor woman's stricken features when all was revealed! Standing up front beside Dave, where *Babette* belonged, and not having had a clue this entire time. It was enough to shrivel you right up in your skin.

Oh, she tried to brush off pity. *Who cares what those tosswads think, anyhow?* Except, Babette did. Dearly. Babette always had, with firm no-nonsense concepts like decency and fair play. No more, no more. She gripped the wheel tightly. Her eye was on the prize now and once you did that, funny how all the niceties such as other folk just sort of … trickled away. Hah. You're so *nice*.

Faster. Babette parted the fraying strings of herself and fed in her guilt, experiencing no little relief to be shot of it. *Faster.* More importantly, she threw her anxiety on top for good measure. That wrenching, deep rooted fear that she'd not thought one whit beyond running through those imposing chapel doors. Dave's expression, of a thousand possible expressions; what Dave might do with the situation she handed him. The terrible glory, the ultimate crowning instant when eternity would stop: of shouting "No!" She offloaded it all to the car.

Twelve! The clock struck twelve but there was still time. Still the waffle of form and ceremony to grind through. The bride could hardly sprint her ass down the aisle, could she, not even if she knew what was coming for her.

Better late than never, and Babette had all the time in that great grey-green world that was rushing by her window. No home in her, head to toe, for fear anymore and she felt wild without it, the dusty corners of her life swept clean. Flying along, faster even than the car, like she was dragging its bulk by the steering wheel.

Babette had become an impossibility in ballistics, stripped down to essentials. All that remained was a burning head and a blazing heart, aimed straight at that church, and boy wouldn't she hit like a firework. It still wasn't fast enough.

Screaming in triumph, with joy at the happiness she deserved and would finally take for herself Babette fed the vehicle all she had left and it was fire.

Exiting the chapel in cheering pursuit of the happy couple, guests ignored the scowling priest at the top of the stairs to throw rice, because people are frankly asshats. No skin off their entitled noses to see him down on arthritic knees picking grains from between pavers before the poor birds got at them and sickened.

Brooding season, it was. In gusts of such balmy weather it brought his soul down into his boots to have to roam about with a stick, knocking nests gone cold from the eaves. Leave those in situ and you got the ants, and wasn't the circle of life just right fucking charming?

With every man and his dog trailing the smiling bride and her groom, only the crotchety priest noticed the cheerful, apple green little car. And only then because it rolled into view, bumped up against the church steps and came to a gentle, sad sort of stop.

He scratched the back of his neck with one withered hand, hearing the laughing revellers in the distance. The car was empty, which was odd. Must have gotten away from somebody.

A short story

MOULD

BP GREGORY

MOULD

My best friend was in Pompeii.

I wasn't, of course, or I wouldn't be standing here staring down at a museum display titled "A BLAST FROM THE PAST!!!" A kitsch red LED volcano flickering gently in the background, flinging deep shadows across expressions of abject misery behind a velvet rope for the small children to point sticky fingers at. Speakers rumble in the distance. One little girl bursts into inconsolable howling at the sight; or perhaps it's the ruddy glowering threat that the same's imminent to be visited on us. I like her immensely. Her father carries her out.

In fact, some years before Pompeii's last days came about I had found myself dutifully lugging my scant possessions down the road with tail tucked between my legs; off to marry, of all things. That's what you did back then when your family saw fit to offload you; and should be the match be prestigious enough "*poof!*" you were magically absolved of the past to boot—not even the neighbours could sneer behind closed doors anymore. Far away and footsore, then. Out of sour, miserably small mind and all that.

The distance didn't matter, of course; my best friend and I were soul mates. I never ventured far before I could feel the line drawing me back in, calling me home. Our simpatico a secret treasure; far too precious to sport on your sleeve because so rare, as much then as now. Women don't ever seem to connect, not truly. They've sharp noses for challenge, and too readily recognise and condemn what lurks within. How are you expected to place faith in a mysterious threatening *other* when personal trust barely stretches so far as you could throw yourself?

But we had somehow weathered that giggly, prickly rivalry of youth when any second double-edged friendship can slide into outright envious warfare, sparking bitter feuds to last the ages. I'd no reason on earth to disbelieve we would hobble on together into our decline, achieving that comfortable state where it no longer matters what hell your crumbling shell resembles or how it's dressed.

And then at last two alike minds could tentatively reach out and clasp hands; honouring other, recognising self.

And she … she helped me. My best friend helped me when nobody else could. There'd not been another soul under all the wide skies like her: the natural outcast, the outsider; none other to so much as recognise my peril. Even I ascertained the threat only vaguely. To me it was no more than a dim line of smoke barely noticed, way off in the distance. Who could see harm in the tiny cough of a newly arrived baby?

Afterward, there were never any accusations of crime: where's the point when it burns in every eye until the very air ignites? For decency's sake I had to abandon home and trudge into the unknown to join some fat bastard I'd never met in holy matrimony.

Thus I escaped Pompeii, and so my name has changed over and again along with the multitudes of the living, heaving world. But not so those who were there, left mute and encysted. Not her. And it grieves me deeply to recall how pertly she'd once turned up her nose at donning a nicer dress, at playing along, her flat refusal in short to be any damn thing but herself; because now she never will be.

But she remains my best friend. Our hold is firm. Every time I am squeezed into life, thrust out into the world through blood and muck she is the very first thing I feel: before light, before air. And that's when I remember Pompeii. I even used to hear her murmuring, sealed away down there. So I guess in a way I'm no more than myself, either.

They went and dug up the town—many many years later, of course. Avid for knowledge, sick enough for sensation to go grubbing around in the dirt. They mixed buckets of cold plaster on site, their improvised wooden paddles going round and round in the thin early Mediterranean light. It would have been hard messy work; arm muscles already burning, shoulders stuffed with ache and complaint. Shoes splattered for the wife to shriek at when they got home.

With long thin tools they drilled down to Pompeii's lost people, who cried out with joy at that first hint of sunlight and air. Finally after all this crushing immobile time there came to the buried hope of rescue, of freedom. I heard my best friend, as the drill whined its way through pumice and compressed ash. While flakes of burned building sifted down onto her. Everyone and their lives were down there: my family, all those sullen despised neighbours; and in fact I've recognised familiar contortions in the frozen grimaces at the museum; but I've never heard any of the others. What do I care for them, anyhow? None of them ever helped me.

I heard my friend weeping, too overburdened to bear it.

But those who had not yet managed to go mad sealed down in the dark had another thing coming, for in went the plaster. The merest golden hint of the wild free sky gleaming in—oh sweet heaven yes, deliver us! Do you remember birds? I remember birds—but then a deluge of thick icy cold clotted down the tube and salvation was blotted out. Thrashing in the dark, screams turning to heavy choked gurgles as the narrow space filled.

The cold was so intense that my breath frosted out of my lungs in a rush, painfully colder than the surrounding air. I was sped to hospital where conscientious staff irrigated my abdominal cavity with warm saline and, when I shuddered and flailed awake, rather gleefully announced that I'd been dead for four whole minutes. Gathered excitedly about my bed they were so very proud of resuscitating me, and didn't at all understand why I wept.

I think I tried to rush to my friend and gather her in my arms, straining to pull her from her prison. But four minutes was just not long enough. I still heard her shrieking hysterically for succour, as they all must have screamed; those who waited so long in the dark and ought to have been saved. As the frigid killing cold consumed them. Not only a new sensation but a final one, filling up everything until cold was all there was left, and it went on forever.

As the plaster stiffened so did they; and although I still feel her drawing me home I have heard my best friend's voice no more. She inhabits a hard, silent place in my mind now. And she's so profoundly cold.

And I, who deserved it so much less; I have lived my quiet times over and over. Always plagued with poor circulation, chill at the fingertips, at risk of losing them, I gravitate to warmer climes. Never too close to anybody. I have borne children. I've sat blissfully in the sunlight. I visit the museum countless times, to stand and look on my friend's horror-stricken face.

All I dare hope is that I might well be unto my best friend as she has been to me. And so the unchanging frozen scar on my soul which is forever entombed may, in her, bloom.

TERRY

THE LEFTOVER COFFEE I'd swilled to keep swollen eyelids propped open rummaged about my heart and guts, keen to give 'em a good boot. Always plenty of caffeine handy come the end of a dreary office day, if you knew how to scare it up and could grimace it down cold. Enough to transform the graveyard shift into something tingly and restless.

'My friend.' I snapped to attention as my companion gently interrupted my thoughts. Cripes, I'd been listing off to one side! 'As I'm sure you're aware, it'll be your head and my proverbial ass on a stick should we ever get found out. *Likely* different sticks ... but then again, one can never tell.' A digital "snork" out of the dark, one of his many odd sounds. 'So I suppose the outlook isn't *all* gloom.'

I wasn't oft inclined to listen to Terry so much as boggle shamelessly, but tonight he made quite the point. A pointy end neither of us had admitted until now. 'Why smack my sticky little fingers, eh? Isn't a soul alive out there who ain't *dying* for a piece of you to stick on their mantle.' Nervousness wobbled my bravado.

It was true: hundreds higher up the food chain were slavering for their pound of flesh and stood before me in line. Once our midnight liaisons came to tawdry light the fan would not just be hit but blitzed. But who could resist? When all the clamouring world packed up their notes and toddled off home, flicking out the lights behind, that left the two of us. Me and Terry.

Terry was no more than a lump of screens and servos to look at, hatched with knowledge in place of nescience. He stayed admirably suave in the face of the denizens of day, the whole kit and caboodle who were gagging to discover if artificial intelligence might be *for real* this time. Really real, finally. Namely, had their big bucks been worth it?

Terry had been the child of every sponsor to unveil bottomless pockets, no matter the brand. Three months in and I'd only just mastered blocking out the marketing onslaught that ringed the rosie. I'd been stuck humming jingles twenty four seven for a while there, and it didn't take much of that to scrape the zen from your nerves.

Three months gone! Really? No wonder I was nodding off— *three*! But you could never get tired of good old Terry. He was by far the most fascinating facet of my life; well worth giving up a bit of kip over.

I sat swinging my heels on Director Hardly-Worth-His-Bonus' imitation blackwood desk. Planted my backside right next to the silver framed photograph of his wife, which went much envied about the surrounding cubicles. The Director polished the fingerprints off the glass each night and all, I checked.

Rudy nude—me, that is, not the wife. Having her perfect visage staring down my hams didn't exactly fill me with spangles of joy but I'd it on very good authority, Terry being close to the highest, that the redhead in the glittering border was actually a local dancer of the exotic calibre. No more Director Hardly-Worth's espoused than myself, so we had equal rights to the desk.

Oh yes, I did mention I was starkers, right? That was the funny thing about Terry. Simultaneous, instantaneous access to every brainy database civilisation could furnish, and what were his hobbies? Sly office chitchat, and watching me swan about naked. Sitting, walking, you name it. Naked.

Not even the most lurid mind could turn to filth, though: there was nothing sexual about it. *Couldn't* be. Terry had no hormones, no swinging tackle or possible inclination. He wasn't even a *he*, not really. Quite the odd duck.

Yet here I perched in the quivering buff, on a desk that from beneath my butt was slowly filling the room with the stink of its warming vinyl inlay. Imitation leather. I shook my head. Directors rarely vexed themselves so far as getting the real deal, and boy didn't it age like a dog.

'Can you say what life is?' For something grinding at me through speakers Terry's enunciation was actually quite melodic. The stammering gamut of scientists, blinking painfully as they emerged into the day, often failed to secure airtime beside Terry's cultured tones. He was overstepping his creators already.

'How do you mean?'

Gears clacked loudly. It was sort of equivalent to a sigh. You had to use your imagination a bit. 'Life … well, life creates, does it not?' Spun out so casually but I wondered how such a statement must flash up in his binary brain, as opposed to my runny organic own. 'The number one most important thing of life, what it exists for, is to create; commonly more life, but I think we can manage better than the common. Your people seem to get all bothered over the *semblance* of life as well. Reflections and so on.'

I shrugged; this was so beyond my everyday. 'I suppose.'

Although I'd sat meekly and completely missed the point, as it turned out Terry was pre-empting the debate that had been raging in the streets outside. And he did so without personally needing to hear a peep of it.

By break of day when my tin hero no longer belonged solely to myself, demure in tweed down the back, the world piled in waving tabloid and newsreel. "Prodigy or Processor?" screamed the headlines. Poor, anxious Team Terry saw themselves en route along a long slow nightmare to becoming the next scientific laughing stock.

'How do we *prove* you're alive?' they demanded, scores of academic scalps about to blow right off.

Our dearest brainchild, all brain and no child, took it coolly in stride.

'My gathered friends.' My view may have been blocked but not access to Terry's purr which slunk to all corners of the room, suave as velvet. 'Refrain from polishing those resumes just yet, please. The answer is dreadfully simple, of course, like all good solutions. My friends, I shall paint you my portrait.'

"Preposterous" sprang fully blown into the room but Terry had turned this all the way around and refused to be balked.

'Just imagine,' he reasoned, with his projection at leisure to steamroll across as many interruptions as duty saw fit. 'An original artwork from a thinking, enlightened *un-human* being. Not from some fleshless robot without soul. A masterpiece that even the most intractable chest thumping caveman could recognise as having come from beyond human experience.'

I smothered a snort. Top work, Terry: why not crack open *every* can in the worm factory? Besides, who's to say we'd even be able to perceive the truly alien? Human experience was all we'd ever known.

Gee but it worked a treat, though. Before you could say publicity stunt our gaggle of excited eggheads, who'd hardly know Blake from Warhol, were getting themselves ripped off by art suppliers everywhere. There went the damn budget for this quarter.

Terry had waxed determined to orchestrate the unveiling of the century. Not even I was allowed a pre-peek, which in my learned opinion genuinely sucked cheese, but still I sat and swung my heels and downed those dregs when the lights snapped out. I was determined to stay in the loop.

For instance, when Terry got to moaning over how mere paint wasn't enough, would *never* be enough, I began to bring him ... other things. Some of his requests were bizarre—normally I quite liked bizarre. Only some of *these* made me sick to the stomach to collect, such as that pet store carton, but I persevered. Told myself sternly that they came from a mill anyhow, which was a revolting practice, and they were destined for short pitiful lives.

I kept myself *important*, and it was almost like having just the two of us again.

'More canvas!' Terry would shout with strange electronic glee. 'Let's get this baby firing on all cylinders!'

Other nights he'd be pensive, too damn moody to pick up a brush. Fur fluffed the wrong way like a teenager. Wasn't he meant to be better than us and our follies?

I shifted restlessly. The inlay was ferocious for the first hour of sitting, until it either warmed or my bits went numb. 'So how's it coming along?'

'Doesn't matter,' Terry grumped—well if he was going to be like that, I might as well have stayed home. 'It's *coming*, that's what's important. No such thing as un-creation, is there? Once a thing gets started, my friend, there's no going back.'

Well that was some fine gibberish. My Terry was out to *prove something*. I could smell it. And in my experience, folks getting their beaks rubbed in somebody else's crusade seldom came to hugs and rainbows.

Things were changing, and I couldn't help but rile up. I'd been unable to wash the turps and linseed aroma from my hair for days. Conspicuous splats of blue winked cheerfully off Terry's shining brass, and bristles were permanently mired all over in gobs of drying puce. 'Leave it, leave it,' the scientists gabbled, 'It's *art*.' Some wit—or git—had perched a woolly beret atop Terry's primary storage matrix. As he didn't seem to mind it was left, and sparked a ferocious return of beatnik out in the world.

'Well thanks for sharing, *friend*.' I angrily kicked the filing cabinet, imitation ash, and a second edition of Big Bold Brushwork thumped to the floor. Fine. *Fine*. I left it there.

When launch day finally came about it really seemed Terry and I were the only ones not grinning like a pack of silly hyenas. Whatever Terry's portrait eventually showed itself to be, the presses stood poised to crank it out on tea towels, t-shirts, any t-related merchandise the mind could conceive.

My expression dragged along the carpet, as if anyone cared. And Terry, well. He simply lacked a face to express whatever it was he had bubbling away inside.

Crowning the worst day of my life, Director Hardly-Worth plunked himself ceremoniously down directly in front of me. Swell. That sure did it. It wasn't enough I had to be stuck up the back; that freakishly disproportionate noggin of his was the final nail in my chances of being first to see. I wondered if that whopping great moose head contained the slightest inkling of what use I put his desk to after dark.

While I quietly spluttered and fumed away, my Terry was winding up his speech already.

'Stop!' I wanted to shout. 'Just show *me*! Not this bulk lot of glutted smiles and pompous middle class bellies!'

Sure. Everyone gathered would just *love* to hear the janitor belt that one out. I bit my tongue instead, glared a hole through the moose head and listened.

Terry carried on. That's what we do, isn't it? We carry on like the pork chops we are. ' … All my friends, I give you fresh from the easel something you could never have conceived alone. You made me and I made this, therefore we have brought this about *together*. Now I wish to help you see as I see. I give you my vision of myself. My very first creation!'

People were already clapping, eager beavers, and the flouncy little curtain was dropped. Just like that.

The applause trailed away. Too short by fully a head I struggled to catch a glimpse of what the rest of the room had shot to their feet to gorge their eyes on. Something monumental was taking place, and as usual I was missing out. Mad with frustration I danced on the spot.

But what was this?

Crowds form an interesting dynamic. They become in a sense like a single beast, especially in the grip of strong emotion, and you can *feel* the moment the mood goes bad. Your shoes warn you by backing up real quiet-like, as I was doing. This had ceased being your standard get together for making friends and influencing.

A quick shudder ran through the masses. I'd seen a mutt's skin shiver in just that way, plagued by biting. Paper rustled and it was *loud*, the room closing in, that airless and tight.

Someone near the front row moaned and suddenly, as though to crush the merest possibility of an individual in that crowd, an insane baying went up. They *were* dogs! The entire assemblage of distinguished intellects, celebrities and reporters opened red mouths to the ceiling and to each other and they howled. And howled.

I might have been hollering my lungs out too, in pants pissing fright if I hadn't been struck dumbfounded. Leaving me and my troubles behind the bellowing crowd surged forward, and both artist and creation were buried in the avalanche of tearing fingers and brutal stamping feet.

Now I found my voice. 'Stop!' I screamed, horrified, still not silly enough to step into it. 'Stop! *Terry!*'

Only a single set of ears in the entire heaving mass heard. Director Hardly-Worth, who'd only been a few steps off. He spun around in a way that hardly boded well for me.

The advancing Director's beefy jaws were wide open and eyes rolling, the attack so canine that thoughtless habit saved me. I stopped backing up. After all, my family had always kept dogs. I loved dogs. 'No!' I smacked him on the nose with two fingers—sharp although not hard, strike like the cobra! 'Bad boy!'

Reacting exactly like an errant puppy, luckily for me, the silvered veteran of the stratospheric tax bracket shook his confounded head, eyes welling up reproachfully. He *wasn't* a bad boy, he was a *good boy*! I crossed my arms, frowning. *Oh you are such a bad boy!* So he turned and punched Joe the coffee boy instead.

At full sprint a pack of bewildered security guards crashed through the door and flung themselves on the mob. It wasn't worth helping, and I turned my back sadly. Nice timing, fellas. The show was already over. My Terry and his sodding portrait had been rent into tiny fragments, some of which the wild eyed dignitaries were still masticating madly.

Those coveted mouthfuls would not be surrendered even as the afflicted were getting their asses loaded into paddy wagons. Apparently it made you quite the big man in the pack. A few required pursuing up and down the hall, chortling merrily like it was a grand game and not utterly horrible. They left a rainbow slime of frothy oil paint and saliva to ruin the carpet behind them.

What few scraps I could salvage went into a biscuit tin on my mantelpiece, but there was no way of telling what they'd been. I stopped pawing through them after a while.

That night I crept back to sit on Hardly-Worth's desk, but it was hardly the same. In a rare show of efficiency all effects had already been whisked away, including the picture of Ms Exotic. Downcast, I looked around. The only point of interest remaining was a newspaper, yesterday's news, the crew hadn't quite used it up in wrapping the breakables. I smoothed out the broadsheet on the desk beside me and saw that Terry had been right.

In Japan they already had a "Tomomi" and America were hammering diligently away at "John," determined not to trail out of the gate.

Whatever had been destroyed in this office had hardly been unmade. Could never be *un-created*. It had made its impact on the world and now that influence was spreading. I just wished I could get my head around it, you know?

But I couldn't, and that was that. There was no point me lingering here trying to place the pieces, all alone like Johnny no-friends. So I put my clothes back on, picked up my broom and headed home to finally, *finally* get some sleep.

If you've enjoyed this, please read on for special bonus short story *Lunchbox*.

lunchbox

BP GREGORY

LUNCHBOX

WE ENDED UP going to a place I knew. John wasn't sure if the bars he used to lurk about were still cool, or even open.

The cold air shocked him back to his senses, some. As we stumbled through a back street labyrinth you could see suspicion prodding with queries he ought to have blurted long before setting foot outside his front door. *Just how well do you know your old buddy Charlie these days?*

But the rose stained lure of good times? You can't beat that.

We swung off into somebody's yard. Somebody who'd once had kids but maybe not now, maybe not for a long time. Either way the parents hadn't had the heart to get rid of their things, and in the dark John grunted and tripped on toys scattered across the concrete square.

Reaching the miniature swing set I swung back and forth, grinning up at tonight's partner in crime. 'It's been too long.'

The entire structure creaked and groaned alarmingly.

'We'll need the Jaws of Life to prise your arse outta that seat,' John observed unkindly. 'Ages four to twelve it says on the side. What are we doing here, Charles?'

Giggling a little I struggled up but the seat came with me, chains rattling. 'Oh crap, I am stuck!' A moment of panic before good old John managed to prise the four-to-twelve plastic off my adult hams.

'Sh!' He cased the house nervously, though all windows remained dark. 'You'll wake the family!'

'Not bloody likely.' I wrestled with one of those rocking horseys that lurch back and forth on springs. The jolly beastie inviting some kid to leap into its saddle sported a stubby horn jutting from its face. It had once been uncomfortably long and wicked before a wiser soul had sawn the plastic down. 'Help me with this.'

John loaned twiglet arms to the effort. 'Why are we stealing this?' he hiss-whispered wetly in my ear, the way tipsy folk think they're being quiet. 'It's hardly gonna match your sofa.'

'Not stealing,' I grunted. 'Push to the left.' Which ought to have done naught, the springs deep seated in concrete, but which nonetheless yielded a deep mechanical click. The entire slab we were standing on grated off to one side.

John leaped away with a thin girlish shriek he tried instantly to cover by coughing.

I bowed, gesturing him down the revealed staircase. 'Aaand welcome.'

'What the hell, Charles!'

'Hey, we're celebrating. What with my being suddenly un-married and all, and you offering to share your spooky secret I'm of a mind to dip my lip in something special.'

The pinkly lit space we dropped down into could loosely be described as a bunker, although the remnants of wall brackets attested it'd been machinery that cowered down here, not people. Now it was crowded with any old arcana that someone had thought looked posh.

'Chaar-leei!' the bartender hollered, a stringy fellow with less gristle than John and not even so tall. Welcoming us he could scarce peep over his own bar.

'Sanjay!' I boomed back, shoving my way to a stool with John along for the ride. 'Break out the fancy pants, I'm treating my friend tonight. We're off to see a ghost!'

'Ghosts, now.' Sanjay rolled expressive eyes, dark as poured obsidian. 'What excuse will you drag in next? Armageddon?' The obligatory pretty young things pulling pints to either side, a lad and a lass, smiled weakly.

Flashing pretty was a cheap stunt to get sad bastards queuing on a mission to drink their egos up, but if you drool more fool you. It was the same worn out dog of a trick everyone used.

At least Uncle Sanjay ensured these kids buckled down; they could run their own establishment someday, books to stock. And he kept them more virtuous than his own blood.

'Bric 'n Brac,' he introduced with a flip of long fingers. Sanjay wasn't handing the leggy adolescents' true names out to anyone, even regulars. 'When you want the rarest drop in the city, here is where you come.'

Bric and Brac smirked, right on cue.

Bending to a spigot Sanjay filled two glass thimbles. 'Some say a sip brings immortality. You'll witness the end of days, hey? I've even had punters stagger back in here to swear it gives sleep without dreams, a far more precious commodity.' He hoisted one to let tangerine light spark through. 'I call it Tears of Fools.'

Bitter, the nose insisted. I accepted mine eagerly.

John merely stared at his, set down on the bar in front of him, cloudy with fingerprints. I nudged him a little, annoyed. 'You've never tasted anything like this, mate. It ain't cheap.'

Sanjay squinted through the labial light. 'Your friend is nervous of the yellow death. He's a good lad to take care of his liver. You should treat it like your old mother.'

'I do!' I protested merrily. 'A sherry tipple every night and shandies on Thursdays.'

'Bric, why don't you set the nice man's fears to rest?'

The improbably comely lad, unless they handed them out at kindergarten, had to be skirting the responsible service minimum. He drew a dribble from the tap onto a spoon. Pinching a tealight off the bar he deftly lit it with the tiniest *woomph*, delicate flamelets curling across the surface.

After a moment held up for inspection Bric flicked the spoon into the sink with a curse, shaking scorched fingers.

'Run it under the cold tap,' Sanjay instructed absently. 'You see, friend? Red spells dead, just like my ex-wife's glare, but this burns blue as my girlfriend's beautiful eyes. What better drop to toast the paranormal, hey?'

'Total furphy, guys,' Brac asserted from her side, flaunting that rare ability to work and chat. 'The city'd be wall to wall ghosts if they were real.'

'And how would you tell?' I wiggled my fingers at her, booga-booga style and she wrinkled her nose. Ah, the old charm. 'We could be neck deep in ghosts *right now*.'

'Oh, you'd know.' Bric threw his two cents in. He figured himself all recovered by now, but Sanjay thrust his hand back under the running tap.

'You know the rules, lad. Ten minutes minimum for a burn, even a bee's dick of one. And don't let me catch you sticking ice on it this time, either. Just damages the cells more.'

Brac's sweetly shaped jaw was on the floor. 'You believe in ghosts? Seriously?' Just went to show you could work with someone ever so long and still have a thing to learn.

'Used to live next to one. Ages back.'

'I call bullflop!'

'No, really. And you don't need to see any ghost to know it's there. It makes everything all … horrible. My family went weird. I was off school for weeks, just hiding in my room and it was like they hardly noticed.'

Sanjay looked unimpressed but Brac's peepers were big and round. The expression took her right back to nights of *never* checking beneath the bed, or in the closet. It was better not to know.

Personally I was delighted, really jonesing on the bump in the night shtick. 'Come on, then. Don't spare us the oocy-juicy!'

'Dunno about juicy,' Bric muttered, finally winning free of the tyranny of the sink. The spoon was now cool enough to pop in the dishwasher, giving him time to rake over memories. 'It was my Mum who first acted off.

'I read up, and apparently if you've had a loss a ghost seems to *get* at you more. Mum's brother, my uncle passed away that year. I know she'd been thinking on him a lot, going through photos and such. *Said* it made her realise how important family was. Well, her behaviour didn't back that up, that was for sure.

'I was just a kid, mind. And one day the meat in my lunch sandwich was raw. Just … raw and cold, slapped between two slices of unbuttered bread. I bit into it before I realised—slimy, ugh! I considered eating the bread, nothing more miserable than going hungry. But soggy pink had seeped all through it.

'When I took it home to show her she laughed in this vague, distant way and said, "What a silly Mummy." No shit, I opened my lunchbox the next day and she'd put a rock in it. A rock! And she'd buttered it! Maybe 'cause I'd pointed out the bread thing along with the raw friggin' meat, I don't know.'

Brac stifled a laugh behind her hands. Those eyes said clearly that she knew it wasn't funny.

Bric nodded. 'Sounds silly now, but I cried so hard. All those other kids eating lunches from parents who loved them, and there was me with my buttery rock.'

Now I snorted too, but I hoped my face was full of sympathy.

Sanjay clapped Bric on the shoulder. 'Lad, anytime you're peckish on my watch just say the word. Nobody does good work on an achy belly.'

'Much less a kid. I certainly wasn't getting much out of classes. Stopped even looking in my lunchbox. Safer to just hold it open over a bin and turn my face away from the things that came thumping out. Whatever I heard, I couldn't look.

'It got worse when Dad started acting up, too. Might be brushing his teeth or something, and suddenly he'd start trying to do it backwards. Had his lips sealed over the drain trying to suck back the foam. He froze there and goggled at me until I finished walking by, like *I* was the one freaking *him* out.

'Started watching me at night, too. I'd wake up and he'd be just standing there in my bedroom. In the dark. Watching me. His eyes were wet and I could find the gleam if I looked hard enough, from the little light that crept under the door. Staring. On those nights I don't think he ever blinked.

'And I always blinked. And then he'd be standing somewhere different in the room. No sound. I'd have to find those wet gleams all over again.

'That's when I started staying home. Slept during the day so I could keep up at night, keep Dad out. I couldn't stand him staring at me any longer.

'And that's when I felt it. The cold. A big blast of ice coming through my bedroom wall from next door, like they had the mother of all air conditioners pointed right at me. But you could only feel it here, you know?' He put a hand over his heart. 'I was so *relieved* when I realised. It meant my parents *did* love me after all. It was the ghost doing all this to them.'

He paused, looking down, until waiting became unbearable.

'And ..?' I urged.

'That morning, come sunup I marched straight to Dad and told him we had to move. That there was a ghost next door, and it was messing everything up.

'Dad nodded in this slow underwater way. Deep down he must've known something was skewiff. He was just waiting to be told which way to jump.

'Before the day was out my family was piled in the car with everything we owned, heading off down the street.

'Looking about, it was suddenly obvious to see all the neighbours had gone. We were the last to leave. Being a dumb kid, I took a glance out the back, one final look at home.

'I swear, the ghost house's window had handprints on it like somebody was watching me back. The rest of the pane all dark and burned looking, and two tiny handprints outlined in frost.'

Sanjay gave a low whistle, shaking himself to work the jeebies loose. 'Well I don't know about you lot, but that's the most disquieting shit I ever heard.'

'Cover your ears, then,' Bric continued miserably, all of it tumbling out like poison. 'The worst came when we made it to our new house.

'Mum and Dad were already warming back to normal. Dad got started on a special dinner right away, to make up for all those missed lunches. Mum, well, for days I couldn't open my mouth without her trying to cram food in.

'I ought to have been happy.

'But there in my new room, when I went to unpack my toys they came out of the box with long rusty nails driven into their faces. Each and every one. Every toy I loved.

'I did that. *I* did it. And to this day I've no memory of doing it, or where I even got the nails. None at all.'

Whoa.

I'd have kept that last to myself.

For a while Bric's swimming eyes looked set to bestow the ultimate in tender sympathy, but now … now she looked sick. We all did, and couldn't settle on where to look. Certainly not at Bric, sickest of us all, who must've spilled more than he meant to.

It took a stern sense of reality to return to the hazy friendliness of the bar. Or irreverence.

Raising his glass, John toasted whey-faced Bric. 'To ghosts, hey?'

The others scowled but I hoisted my own drink enthusiastically. 'Neck deep in 'em!'

Going down, the tears of fools scalded like fire.

Lunchbox

Ideas that start out small don't always stay that way.

As it appears here at 2,261 words **Lunchbox** was initially a short piece. Instead of doing what it was told and staying small, it preyed on the mind even after its exorcism onto paper.

It eventually put down roots and grew to become the novel **Something for Everything**.

ALSO BY BP GREGORY

NOVELS

Flora & Jim
The Town
Something for Everything (Automatons Book #2)
Automatons (Automatons Book #1)
Outermen

NOVELLA

Only Skin

SHORT STORY COLLECTIONS

Vu Ja De, Collected Short Stories Volume Three
Orotund, Collected Short Stories Volume Two
Cacophony, Collected Short Stories Volume One

SOMETHING
FOR
EVERYTHING
Automatons Book Two

BP GREGORY

Long ago humanity retreated into migrating cities, leaving the landscape to monsters. Within the safety of walls the caste of Surgeons are denied human touch to preserve their skills.

A Surgeon must not be touched. The city can never stop. Comforting truths to live by. But the other cities have fallen silent. Fear stalks the streets. And John the Surgeon craves touch more than anything.

Monsters, machines and roaming cities, insanity, betrayal and lust: centuries later, the seeds of grim legacy sown in Automatons have borne strange fruit indeed...

KATE KNOWS
WHAT SHE
SAW

The
T**O**WN

BP GREGORY

Kate knows what she saw: a burned out ruin. But the evidence is gone, and nobody else believes the town was ever there.

She knows the town exists. Determined to prove it at any cost, in poking around the outback Kate risks exposing herself and her friends to the slew of horrible urban legends, reticent locals, and too many people who vanished over the years with nowhere to go.

Author and avid reader BP Gregory brings monsters, machines and roaming cities, insanity, betrayal and lust! With such tales you shouldn't always feel comfortable or safe.

For sneak peeks, more stories, reviews and recommendations and she ploughs through her to-read pile visit bpgregory.com.